IT ADDS UP TO TROUBLE

IT ADDS UP
TO TROUBLE

by

Anthony Nuttall

Dales Large Print Books
Long Preston, North Yorkshire,
England.

British Library Cataloguing in Publication Data.

Nuttall, Anthony
    It adds up to trouble.

    A catalogue record for this book is
    available from the British Library

    ISBN 1-85389-906-2 pbk

First published in Great Britain by Robert Hale & Co., 1972

Copyright © 1972 by Anthony Nuttall

The moral right of the author has been asserted

Published in Large Print 1999 by arrangement with Robert
Hale Ltd.

Dales Large Print is an imprint of
Library Magna Books Ltd.
Printed and bound in Great Britain by
T.J. International Ltd., Cornwall, PL28 8RW.

Chapter One

As soon as Christie came back from lunch I thought he would have discovered the theft I'd carried out while he was away. He didn't. Or if he did, he said nothing to me. He just sat in his own office all afternoon while I toiled away on some artwork for a firm called Charmwear; a new account that Christie thought would rake in the money if only we handled it right. By that he meant that I'd get the ideas and do all the work, while he took the credit. At five o'clock I put the drawings away, swept my pens and pencils into the drawer and got my coat on.

'Good night, Mr Christie,' I called.

'Wayne,' he shouted as I was opening the door. 'Have you a minute?'

This is it, I thought and turned back,

bracing myself for the argument I knew was coming. When you're the junior in a two-man advertising agency you can't steal from the boss without there being a fuss afterwards.

I poked my head round the wooden partition which divided his office from where I sat.

'I'd like that Charmwear thing to be ready early next week,' he said.

I was so surprised that all I did was stare at him. He had a round, red face and stringy white hair. If you painted a football red and dropped a mop head over it you'd have a good imitation of him.

'I'll see what I can do,' I said, and turned away.

He didn't call me back. I went home, had some tea and then got out the car again. Marie Atkinson, my girlfriend, didn't live very far away, and though she wasn't expecting me I reckoned that she'd be in. She was. Her face didn't exactly come alight when she saw me, but she looked cheerful enough.

'I didn't think you were coming round tonight, Wayne.'

'Neither did I until lunchtime.' I leaned on the door, banging it shut, and then tossed her an envelope.

'What's this?' she asked.

'Open it and see.'

She tore it open, using one of her long fingernails as a paper knife. She's the kind of girl who can get you where it matters without speaking a word or even looking at you. She's about my height, with dark hair that falls in a frame on each side of her face, and right now she was wearing a black dress with a white belt. The dress was so short and the neckline so plunging that I was surprised the top and bottom didn't meet in the middle.

She took out the photograph that was in the envelope and stared at it. Her face went as white as Christie's hair.

'Where did you get this?' she asked in a husky voice.

'It came into the office with a packet of other stuff from Maurice Longford. Christie sells pictures like that to his mates at a quid a time.'

'You don't mean you bought it off him?'

'I stole it,' I said harshly. 'I stole the whole bloody dozen of them.'

I dropped into a chair while she stood by the fireplace, holding the photo by one corner and staring at me.

'I'd have given you some,' she began. 'There was no need to steal—'

'I don't want the damned things!' I yelled at her. 'I don't want Christie to have them either.'

A lad had brought them just before lunch, in a flat, sealed packet. I knew they were of Marie, who does occasional modelling for us, and I wanted to have a look at them. I couldn't open the packet without Christie's knowing and I knew from things he'd said in the past that he doesn't think much of Marie. I don't know why, but to save argument I never pressed the point, nor did I tell him when I actually started going around with her.

I handed him the packet, expecting that he'd have a look at them. When he took it off me without a word and slid it into the top drawer of his desk I was a little fazed.

'Are you sure they'll do, Mr Christie?' I asked.

'Yeah,' he said. 'They'll do. Longford wouldn't send me stuff that's no use.'

There was nothing else that I could say then but when he went to lunch about quarter of an hour later I went round the partition again and pulled open the drawer. It was full of old pencils, a few cheap scribbling blocks that he used to work out his half-baked ideas on before giving them to me to polish up, and a box of drawing pins. No packet of photos. I slammed the drawer shut and lit a cigarette, wondering what he could have done with it. There was no reason I knew of why he should have taken it out with him, and the only other thing I could think of was that he'd deliberately hidden it so that I wouldn't be able to have a look.

The thought sent a surge of annoyance through me, and I began to go carefully through the filing cabinets and drawers, determined now to find them. It wouldn't have been so bad if he'd had any right to interfere between me and Marie. He hadn't, and the fact that he was doing only made me more determined to go against him and do what I wanted to, not what he thought best.

I was going to look at those pictures, and then to drive home the point I was going to leave them in the middle of his desk. If he said anything about it, or told me again that I would be better off having nothing to do with her, I would push them down his throat.

I found them at last, in the bottom

drawer of the filing cabinet. The packet had been opened, and I sat down in his chair and tipped out the photos. They were all ten-by-eights, except for a dozen or so postcards at the back, held together with a rubber band.

It was these which attracted my attention. They were of Marie and she was naked in every one of them. They were the kind of pictures that I wouldn't have had in the house, not even to light the fire with, though if I'd used them for that they'd have been very economical. They were so red-hot that I would have needed neither matches nor coal.

'What did you do with the others?' Marie asked abruptly, jerking me back to the present. 'There's only one in this envelope.'

'I'd have liked to have made Christie eat the damned things,' I growled. 'I dropped them down a grid instead.'

'How many were there?'

'A dozen or so. With what he charges

and the repeat orders he gets I'd say there was a hundred quids worth.'

She didn't speak.

'Not a very nice thing to find your girlfriend doing, is it?' I demanded. 'I didn't think that pansy Langford went in for stuff like this. Is that how he got his big car?'

She dropped the photo onto the floor and stamped on it. Her heel punched a hole right through it.

'I've got to get money somehow, Wayne.'

'Not like that.'

'How else? I get paid well for them.'

'That's all you ever think about,' I sneered. 'Money, money, money. If you had your way you'd turn me into a five pound note and spend me.'

'Wayne—'

'Don't pose for anything like that again,' I said, raising my voice. 'Especially not with Longford. I hate him. If I ever find—'

'Wayne Edwards,' she broke in, her

voice cutting across mine with all the force of a railway engine's horn competing with a trumpet, 'Tell me one thing. How long have you owned me? I'll do what I like. If I get offers like that, as well as ordinary modelling, I'll take them. I'm going to do a film, soon, as well.'

'A film?' My throat had gone dry.

She nodded.

'Like that?' I asked, pointing to the skewered photo.

'I guess so.' She shrugged. 'It depends what Maurice wants.'

'I may have pulped all his bones by then.'

'If I want to do it, I will!' she flared. 'He's paying me more for it than you earn in a month. The only thing that's going to stop me is something that pays me more money.'

'Like what?' I jeered. 'The only thing that'll ever give you enough money is a printing press.'

'It's up to you to find a way if you

want to stop me,' she said casually. 'I thought you'd know all about those pictures, working for Christie, or doesn't he think you're old enough to be told? Maybe he's right.'

'Now listen, honey—'

'You listen to me,' she said. 'If I want to do that sort of work, I will. It pays well, and it's fun, but if you can find something that pays better I'll pass up the fun. It's up to you, Wayne.'

II

Christie didn't mention the missing photos to me, and as far as I was aware no one brought any others. Of course, he could easily have slipped round to see Longford himself, or have had them delivered while I was out, but I wasn't bothered because I didn't know about that.

Besides, I was thinking too much about what Marie had said about making more money.

The only thing I could think of was to bite Christie's ear for a few more quid a month. After all, I was practically carrying his agency and he knew it, and he'd introduced me to Marie so it was only fair that he should help to finance her.

It had been a freezing cold day in Hyde Park and, typically, we had been doing some photos for a line of soft drink adverts to go out that summer. As soon as I'd seen Marie I'd felt as if a bomb had been touched off underneath me, but she didn't seem to notice that I was there. She was too busy looking the other way, trying to spot the photographer, who was nearly a quarter of an hour behind time.

'I've never known Maurice be as late as this,' she'd said suddenly.

'Quit worrying.' Christie obviously hadn't been as smitten by her as I was. 'You're being paid for your time so why should you worry about how late he is?'

'I'm thinking of all the other things I could be doing,' she'd snapped. 'And the work I'll lose if I'm ill after hanging about in the cold.'

Christie had laughed.

'I shouldn't worry about that, either. I don't reckon you'll starve.'

She hadn't replied to that. Her face had gone nearly as red as his and she'd turned away from him. Seeing as that had brought her round to look at me I didn't bother, and I'd smiled at her stony face.

'Isn't that Longford coming now?' I'd said, to break the uncomfortable silence.

It was, too. I hadn't seen much of him before that, but I couldn't forget his mincing walk and his curious way of speaking, as if his words had been flattened in a press before being allowed out of his mouth. He'd minced up to us, throwing one end of his purple muffler over his shoulder and putting his camera bag on the ground.

'Hope I didn't keep you waiting,' he'd said. 'The phone rang as I was leaving and I was tied up in another assignment.'

'You'll need all the other assignments you can get if you keep me hanging about in weather like this,' Christie had growled. 'Let's get on with it now that you've decided to turn up.'

In a thin summer dress Marie had looked even more sensational. Even though the weather was so bitter and she'd been snuggling into a fur coat before Longford's arrival, she didn't seem to feel the cold once she was working. She'd posed this way and that with various dummy cartons and bottles of the soft drink, appearing to knock the stuff back as if she lived on it, and Longford had minced around with his meters and so on, the ends of his purple scarf constantly getting in his way but not seeming to bother him too much.

After one of the shots, Marie had brushed against me, and I still hadn't got over the feeling, nor the way she'd smiled at me, when we'd got back to the crummy office that Christie rented.

He must have seen the way I'd been

looking at her, because as he unlocked the door and trampled over a couple of circulars that were lying on the mat he'd said:

'I wouldn't get too worked up over that bird, kid, if I were you.'

'Which bird is that, Mr Christie?' I'd asked, keeping my face turned away from him so that he wouldn't see that my expression didn't match the casual tone of voice that I managed to use.

He'd banged his hands together and stood in front of the electric fire.

'Marie Atkinson,' he'd said. 'I saw the way you were looking at her.'

I could tell from the tone of his voice that he was leering as he said that, but I still hadn't looked towards him or shown any sign that I was bothered about what he was saying.

'I think you're wrong,' I said.

'I think I'm right.' He'd walked round to where I couldn't help having to look at him but by then I was more in control of what I was doing. 'She's rotten, kid. Rotten all through. You can tell that just by looking at her.'

'I'm not interested in her,' I'd said pointedly, going over to my desk and sitting down.

'Leave her to Longford,' he'd advised me.

Longford was the photographer we'd just been working with, a pansy character with a shining new Mercedes which contrasted oddly with Christie's wreck.

'There's a punk I wouldn't mind seeing come a cropper,' Christie had gone on, 'but you're different. In this game you meet a lot of queer characters, and they're two of them.'

'You seem to know a lot about her.'

'I know more than you do, kid. Take my word for it, she's rotten. She'll kill someone before she's through and I'd rather it be Longford than you.'

'You've got me wrong, Mr Christie,' I'd said, smiling, trying to make a joke of it, though the muscles on my face were so stiff that they might have been in a freezer for a week. 'I'm not worried about her.'

'Well, let it drop now,' he said, and went round the partition which gives him a semblance of a private office.

I stared at the green painted wood, then worked for about twenty minutes. When I found that I couldn't concentrate I got up and went over to the phone book.

Christie came out right when I'd found Marie's name.

I dropped the book as if it had closed and tried to snap off my hand.

'You'd do better to forget her,' he'd said, with a knowing smile on his red face.

'I reckon you're the one who wants to forget her!' I'd cried, suddenly annoyed with the way he'd kept going on. 'You've never stopped talking about her since we came back. Even if I do fancy her, it's nothing to do with you!'

She hadn't been mentioned in the office since, but that was why I didn't tell

Christie when I actually took her out, and why he wouldn't let me see those pictures. As far as he knew, I'd forgotten about her and that was the end of it.

On the first night out with her we left her flat and began to walk to the cinema we'd arranged to go to, following it up with a restaurant. When we'd been walking for a couple of minutes she'd said:

'You parked your car far enough away from the flats, didn't you?'

'I don't have a car,' I'd said.

'Oh.'

That was all she'd said. Nothing else, though she looked thoughtful for a long time afterwards and I wished that I'd had the sense to at least hire one for the evening. When we came out of the restaurant it was raining and we had to run across to a taxi rank and wait a few minutes for a cab to turn up. During the wait I could see her getting more and more irritable, and sweat was mingling with the rain on my face when one finally swung round the corner and stopped alongside us. Marie had jumped in almost before the door was properly open and flopped onto the seat.

I'd given the driver her address and moved close to her.

'I'm thinking of getting a car,' I'd said. 'One something like that Mercedes of Maurice Longford's would suit me.'

She'd swung round to face me, an angry expression on her face.

'Maurice is a creep,' she'd said furiously, 'and I wish you'd keep quiet about him. It's you I'm out with, Wayne. If I'd wanted to talk about him I'd have gone one better and let him take me out instead. Now let him drop.'

I'd have liked to have let him drop, but not the way she meant.

'When are you thinking of getting your car?' she asked casually when we'd got back to her place.

The first I'd thought of it had been in the taxi coming back here, but I hadn't told her that. I couldn't really afford a car on what Christie paid me, but there was little point in telling her that, either.

'Perhaps in a week or two,' I'd said.

'Make it soon, Wayne. It's not that I mind walking, but you're so restricted without a car.' She'd giggled suddenly. 'And I know a lot of games you can play in a car.'

By the middle of the following week, I'd had a car. I couldn't really afford it but Marie was suitably impressed and that was all I was worried about. Everything was fine for another week or so, and though her talk of how much she saw of Longford during the day sent an occasional twinge of jealousy through me there had been nothing to worry about.

And then I'd found the photographs.

I hadn't realized that was how she was seeing Longford, and I'd been good and mad. Now I had to think up a way of getting some more money, or I was sure I'd lose her. I didn't want that but I was still no nearer the money two days later, when Christie asked me if the Charmwear stuff was ready yet.

'Half an hour,' I said.

'Bannister's been on. He'd like them as soon as possible.'

Bannister was the big shot at Charmwear.

'I'll see what I can do,' I said. 'Is he sending somebody round for them?'

Christie shook his head. His hair trembled from side to side like a mop in a high wind.

'He wants you to take them round to his house as soon as they're ready. Borrow my car if you like.'

I'd thought it would be tactless to turn up at the office in a car I'd just bought and then tell Christie that I couldn't manage on my salary, so he didn't know about that either, and a while later I was driving Christie's heap up to Bannister's front door.

He lived in one of those big places, like a whole block knocked into one and dropped into the middle of a park, and Christie's car creaked up the drive to the accompaniment of a sneering look from the gardener, who leaned on his rake and watched me. I stopped outside the door and got out.

'Hey!' he called, coming over slowly. 'You can't leave that car there. See that oil it's dripping over the gravel.'

'So what do you want to do about it?' I demanded. 'Lie under it with your finger on the hole?' I'd already been soundly beaten in a burn up with a girl in a sports car who'd laughed as she passed me in third gear, and had to listen to some wisecracks from a couple of punks at some traffic lights, so I wasn't in any mood for this.

'There's no need for that,' he said. 'Just back it up round the side.'

I did as he said, making him jump to one side as I swung backwards, then I got out again and rang the bell.

The door was opened by a trim bird in

a black skirt and white blouse.

I told her who I was and what I wanted. She told me to come in and then closed the door after me.

'Mr Bannister will be free in about half an hour,' she said.

By now I'd had enough of this house. It may have been my imagination but the hall was so big that I fancied I could hear her voice echoing as she spoke.

'Look, baby,' I said, 'these things are urgent. You'd better tell Mr Bannister that I've come all the way from London under the impression that he wanted them right away. I haven't got time to sit around until he thinks he's ready.'

Maybe I wasn't the world's best salesman but then, Christie's car wasn't the world's best car, and I'd been driving it for too long. Fighting was more the word. The girl ran her tongue over her lips and glanced towards one of the closed doors which I could see beyond the hall.

'Is he in there?' I asked.

She nodded.

'I'll see him now,' I said, pushing past her as she tried to stop me.

'Come back,' she called urgently. 'You can't go in there.'

But I was already knocking on the door and when a deep voice called for me to come in I turned the handle and did just that.

Bannister was big and hairy. He looked like a bear dressed in a pale blue suit. With him in it, even one of these huge rooms shrank to a normal size and the furnishing, which had seemed heavy and clumsy, now looked a mite frail for someone as big as he was.

My eyes slid away from him to the table which he was bending over. On the table was a lamp and in the light of that lamp the heap of diamonds which he was poking with his fat, hairy forefinger glittered and twinkled so brilliantly that I was dazzled for the moment.

III

After the way I'd barged into Bannister's room I'd expected trouble. Funnily enough, he was surprisingly mild, though he shovelled the diamonds into a safe fast enough and turned the key, leaving it in the lock. We spent an hour or so going through the designs, then he said that he'd put them to his own people and I left, leaving only the smear of oil on the gravel as a trace of my visit.

The sight of the diamonds had excited me. I thought about them all the way back to London, wondering where he'd got them, why he needed them and what he intended to do with them. They were still coming in and out of my mind a couple of days after, though I hadn't mentioned them to anyone else, not even Marie. I don't know why not; at that time there was no definite idea in my mind.

When I was out with her later that week, we saw Maurice Longford in a restaurant.

I wasn't sure whether or not he'd spotted us, but Marie kept an eye on him and said that she was pretty certain he hadn't noticed that we were there. Even so, I was glad when we left. I hated Longford, though I'd only spoken to him once, and the sight of him only a few feet away from me made me feel cold and sent a strange, prickly feeling up and down my spine.

Marie had been on to me quite a few times, telling me how much money he had and how he used to spend it on the girls he took out. I knew that she'd been out with him more than once, and that he'd given her an expensive present the previous Christmas. I knew that he'd first got her to pose for those pictures one night when she'd been so drunk that she'd hardly dared speak for fear it might spill out of her mouth. Afterwards, of course, she'd done it for a fee and although there hadn't been any mention of it since the night we'd had that argument I knew that there'd been at least one session since, and that the time for her to make that film was drawing nearer.

And I still had no more money.

When I got paid that month, I'd made up my mind to see Christie. I knew that I wouldn't get much from him, but it would be a start at least.

Things didn't work out quite that way.

He gave me the little brown envelope, fat with the pound notes inside it, and then went out as I slit it open. There were thirteen pounds short of what I usually get. I counted them twice, to make sure, and then looked at the slip he gives me to show deductions; there was nothing on it other than the normal tax and so on, and when he came back I went into his office.

'I don't think my wages are right, Mr Christie,' I said, looking worried in case he thought that it was some sort of con to get more money out of him.

'What's the matter with them, kid?'

'You haven't given me enough,' I said. 'I make it that there's thirteen pounds short.'

He gave me a funny little smile, leaning back, his hands behind his head and his red face aglow with suppressed enjoyment.

'Thirteen quid, eh, Wayne? That's a lot of money.'

'That's right,' I said, sensing that something was going wrong but not sure what it was.

'That's what it cost me for those photographs you stole,' he said.

I opened my mouth to say something, then thought better of it and closed it again.

'I always thought it was you,' he went on, 'but I didn't have any proof until the other day.'

'And what proof have you got now?' I asked savagely.

'Maurice Longford saw you with Marie,' he said. 'I can put two and two together, kid. I always said she was rotten and it shows I'm right. She's already turned you into a thief.'

'Now look—'

'We'll forget it now, shall we?' he said.

'No we won't,' I said, glad somehow that everything was now out in the open. 'If you hawk stuff like that around you can't complain if people who don't like it rip it up.'

I leaned over and pulled out the drawer of his desk. There was a bundle of photos in it. I snatched them out before he could stop me and took the top few out of the broad rubber band which held them. They were much the same as the ones of Marie, only of a couple of girls I didn't know who smiled up at me, their mouths inviting but a curious blankness about their eyes as if they didn't know what they were doing or where they were.

Probably they didn't.

Christie stared at me, and his face turned even redder than usual as I tore the photos across and across and flung the bits at him.

I told him what I thought of his rotten agency. I told him that as far as I was

34

concerned I'd finished, I'd had enough. I got my coat on and walked out.

For a while I walked around the streets, ignoring the thronging crowds, a lot of them holidaymakers, happy and cheerful, some of them teenagers prowling about, a desperate look in their eyes as they sought for the swinging London they'd been told existed, and couldn't find it.

So I was out of a job. I had to live, and there was the rent on the flat and the car payments to keep up. I hadn't really been able to afford them before, and I knew that it was something I'd be better off without for a few weeks, but I also knew something else. If I didn't have the car I'd lose Marie for sure, and I would rather have had anything happen but that.

Not that I anticipated much trouble in getting another job. There were plenty of other advertising agencies, most of them better than Christie's, and if I'd thought that there'd have been any trouble finding a job with one of them I wouldn't have left

Christie in such a hurry. That was what I told myself then, and Marie later, but although she seemed to agree with me I saw a calculating look come into her hard little eyes, as if she was working out how long the money she knew I had would last before it ran out.

The day after I started to work my way through the classified list of agencies, phoning each one in turn, asking if they wanted any staff. A couple of them were interested, but when I told them I'd been with Christie they cooled off; I don't know why that was because he hasn't got all that bad a reputation in the business. In fact, I don't think he had any reputation at all, which was maybe what bothered them.

By the time I got halfway down the list I was so desperate that I'd have swept the floor for them, reckoning to work my way up afterwards, but at the one I suggested that to I was told distantly that all their office cleaning was put out to contract.

'Thanks very much, baby,' I said to

the girl, baring my teeth into the phone. 'That's a big help.'

A week later, I was still out of work. The car was paid up for another fortnight, the rent for another three weeks, so there was no immediate worry about that; I cut down on my other spending by cadging meals off Marie, but I could see that cooking for the pair of us after a hard day's modelling didn't thrill her too much.

'You'll have to get some money, Wayne,' she said, one of the nights. 'We can't go on like this. I'd lend you some but I haven't all that much myself.'

'I wouldn't take it off you,' I said, which was true.

A week later, things were getting desperate. In spite of the amount she was paid for her work, Marie didn't really have all that much tucked away, and my own savings were on the point of vanishing. I suggested jokingly that I might sell the car, but the freezing look I got told me that wasn't even a starter.

The job situation was just the same, and I felt it wasn't going to alter, or at least not so's I'd notice. I'd heard nothing at all from Christie, either, but I hadn't been expecting to; there was an envelope with just my insurance card in, but that had been all.

'Maurice might lend you something,' Marie said.

I'd never actually told her the true cause of the row with Christie.

'I wouldn't borrow off Longford,' I told her. 'I hate him.'

She shrugged.

'So do I, but I still work for him. I can't afford to be that choosy.'

'He'd laugh if I asked him,' I said. 'He's a mate of Christie's. He'd rather see me die than lend me money. If I asked him, they'd fall about at the thought of it when they got together over a pint.'

We left it there. Two nights later she went out with Longford. She said that it was to do with her job, to discuss some series of fashion photos they were going to shoot, but I knew her better than that. I spent the evening in my lonely flat, cold because I didn't want to spend money by putting the fire on, and when I rang her flat at half past midnight she still hadn't come in. Just to be awkward I tried Longford's place too, but there was no answer there either, and by the time I'd spent the night in a horrible condition that was neither asleep nor awake I wasn't in any mood to think about anything sensibly.

I had to have money, big money, not the peanuts I'd been messing with up to now, and I had to have it quickly.

It was while I was buttering a couple of slices of toast that I thought of those diamonds at Bannister's house.

Chapter Two

'Are you sure they were diamonds?' Marie asked when I told her about it that night, 'and not imitation or something like that?'

'Honey,' I said, 'a punk like Bannister doesn't have imitation anything. If they looked like diamonds, and they did, then that's what they were. Don't worry on that score.'

I'd thought about it all day before finally deciding to tell her. In the end, I knew that if I was going to make a success of it I'd have to have help, and she was about the only person I could trust; in addition, I thought she might be able to find me a particular kind of help that I hadn't a clue how to set about finding for myself.

She'd taken it better than I'd thought, but then, she always took things well if they promised her money at the end.

'We'll have to get the details settled,' I said. 'One of the things we want to know is how we're going to get rid of them.'

'Don't worry about that,' Marie said. 'In my racket I meet a load of people. I think I can find someone who'll give you good money for them.'

'Who?' I asked suspiciously.

'I don't know yet, do I? I'll let you know when I've got it all fixed up.'

'You'll have to be careful,' I said, worried a little now that she might say too much to the wrong people and give us away before we'd started.

'Look, Wayne,' she said, coming to sit next to me on the settee. 'I'm not that stupid. You'll have to leave this to me. Do you know anyone who could get rid of them without bringing the cops running round?'

I shook my head, and then stared back at the television screen where a couple of hicks were reciting some patter that they seemed to think was funny. I didn't think it was funny, but in the mood I was in then the only thing that would have made me laugh would have been watching Christie and Longford fall out of a high window and break their damned necks.

Marie was still talking about getting rid of the diamonds.

'Even if I told you the people to go to,' she said, 'they wouldn't deal with you because they'll think you're a plant from the cops. You wouldn't believe how careful they are who they talk to.'

Marie was the kind who could make the Sphinx sit up on its hind legs and yap its head off, and I'd known that I was right when I'd thought she could find me someone like that.

'The other thing we'll have to have is information,' I went on. 'We want to know if the diamonds are still there, how many people there are in the house, why he keeps the stuff in the first place.'

She looked a bit startled at that but

merely nodded her head and said that she'd get someone who might be able to find out things like that. I didn't see her the following day. Nor did I see her the day after, and by the time I rung her bell that evening I'd had plenty of time to think about it, and was about ready to call everything off. The difficulties seemed too much for me to cope with, and there was always the snag that the cops might find out too much and come round to see me. That frightened me more than anything and the thought of sitting cooped up in a cell, day after day, week after week, perhaps for years, made me break out into a sweat. Marie would be involved too, and that would be worse. Not only would she blame me for everything but by the time she came out she wouldn't be good for anything. No. It had to be called off, and fast, before the idea of all that money became rooted too deeply in her mind.

I prodded the bellpush.

She smiled at me as she opened the door, but didn't speak. I tried to imagine her beautiful young face and figure after a couple of years of prison, and my mouth went dry.

She narrowed her eyes.

'Is something wrong?'

'No,' I said, surprised at the hoarseness of my voice. 'I've been hurrying. I could use a drink.'

I went into the flat and then stopped. Sitting on the settee, where I usually sit, was a stranger. He was about my age. He looked big, but no bigger than a fair sized gorilla, and his shoulders were no wider than a barn door. His hair swept over his head and covered his ears, contrasting oddly with a pale and completely hairless chin. He wore trousers which were coloured red and green and yellow in half-inch wide stripes, a purple shirt with a big roll collar, and a necktie which was six inches wide at the bottom with a picture of Rupert Bear transferred on it and the words 'Mr Singer is here' printed around it.

Marie said to me: 'I want you to meet Mr Singer.' She didn't bat an eyelid, but maybe she was used to him.

'What else do I call you?' I said.

'How do you mean?'

'I don't go for this mister jazz. I like things to be nice and friendly.'

'You call me mister and like it,' he said. 'I like things to be respectful.'

I looked at him thoughtfully. Apart from being bigger than me he had a hard, ratty face and his eyes glittered out of it like two highly polished currants. In spite of the Rupert Bear and the fancy dress I knew instinctively that he was a tough, dangerous punk who'd think no more of snapping me in two across his knee than I would of swatting a fly.

I sat down on one of the chairs.

'What's with Rupert?' I asked, trying to be cheerful.

'I like him,' he said, watching me expressionlessly, like a currant bun waiting for you to eat it. 'Want to make something of it?'

'No, no,' I said hastily. 'I was just interested.'

'Marie tells me you've got a proposition,' he said, glancing at her. 'Something about some diamonds.'

I swallowed. If I was going to back out, that was the moment to do it but for some reason I couldn't see myself telling that joker that he'd wasted his time by coming here. I could have taken a chance regardless, of course, but if I had he'd probably have done something playful in reply, like pasting my head against the wall. Just to show that there were no ill feelings.

'Yeah,' I said. 'Some diamonds.'

'How many?'

'Worth maybe thirty thousand on the legitimate market.' One of the advantages of working in advertising was that you picked up a lot of odd, unrelated facts about all kinds of things, and I'd been able to work out the value of those stones to within a couple of thousand.

'So I'd be able to get about twenty thousand for them,' Singer was saying. 'Not a fortune but it'll do to be going on with.'

It was a fortune to me but I didn't argue with him.

'Maybe you'll pay me five grand,' he said.

'Two,' I said, not looking at him.

'What's that?'

'You heard,' I said curtly.

Marie's eyes were wide and staring and I could see that although she would never have admitted it she was scared of him. I'll agree that if I'd been going on a walking holiday in lonely country there are people I'd rather have taken with me, but I wanted him to see that he wasn't going to get it all his own way.

'Five grand,' he said softly. 'Otherwise

47

I don't work with you and you'll have wasted my time.'

He made it sound as if wasting his time was only one step short of murder. Probably it was—for him.

'And what will you do for that?' I sneered.

'Get you all the information you'll need and get rid of the stuff afterwards for you. There'll be no come-back from the cops and I'll get you a better price than you'll get from anyone else.'

I said: 'What happens if there turns out to be no diamonds?'

He stiffened.

'What?'

'I've seen them once, about two weeks ago, but that doesn't mean they're still there, or that he's got a fresh lot. I won't be able to pay you anything if they've gone.'

He smiled and looked from me to Marie and back again. When his eyes were off her, Marie shuddered, and I wondered how she'd come to pick up a creep like him.

'We'll sort that out if I find that they've gone,' he said. 'We'll come to some arrangement.' He smiled as he said it, but I wasn't very impressed. I began to hope and pray that the diamonds would be there and when he'd gone I asked Marie what she thought she was playing at, getting us involved with someone like that.

'You won't find anyone better,' she said. 'He'll do what he says.'

'That's what I'm worried about. He's dangerous, honey, make no mistake about that. I'd rather look for a penny in a box of rattlesnakes than argue with him.'

'You shouldn't have to do either if things work out all right,' she told me. 'Now let's try and forget him, shall we?'

II

We saw Singer again a few nights later. He was sitting on the settee as silently as before, waiting for me to arrive at Marie's flat. He grinned as I came in and flexed his fingers that put me in mind of a couple of bunches of bananas. This time, the striped trousers had gone, though the yellow jeans and apple green shirt weren't much better. I guess the Rupert Bear head carefully drawn on the shirt pocket was inevitable, but I personally wouldn't have had it done in luminous inks; still, that was his worry and as long as I didn't have to look at him too much I didn't care.

'Well?' I said, my voice brittle. 'What's new?'

'You're in luck,' he said, sprawling out on the settee. 'The diamonds are there. All you've got to do is walk in and take them.'

'Why does he have them there?'

'As far as I can find out, it's some sort of tax fraud. That should make it even easier for you because he won't be too anxious to get the cops in on a thing like that.'

'I suppose not. Where are they? In that downstairs safe?'

'That's right,' Singer said with a nod. 'And there's only him in the house.'

'Are you sure? The place is big enough to hold an army.'

'There's only him,' Singer repeated, looking at me with a funny glint in his eyes. 'He works from there. Sometimes he has a lot of people to put up overnight. That's why the place is so big.'

'I hope you're right.'

'You're paying me five thousand quid to be right.'

'How did you find out?' I asked curiously.

'That's nothing to do with you. As long as I've got you the gen without involving your name, that's all you need worry about.'

We were coming to the tricky part now, and I went over to the cupboard and poured myself a drink before I started on it. Singer watched me but he didn't ask for anything himself and neither did Marie. All she did was sit on the arm of the chair, staring at Singer like a cat at a rabbit, and occasionally swinging her foot from side to side.

'I'm going to need some help,' I said casually.

'What kind of help?' he asked, his eyes narrowing.

'Someone to look out for any trouble, to help me get into the house, that sort of thing.'

'Not my line, pal. You'll have to cut someone else in if you want that.'

I tossed down some of the whisky and went to sit opposite him.

'I don't want anyone else in on this,' I said. 'It's all eating into the profits and adding to the risk. I wouldn't have brought you into it but I had to get the details some way. I'd like to keep it between the three of us.'

'I'm not messing with it,' Singer said. 'I've already stuck my neck out by asking the questions. If anything does go wrong the cops are going to come right to my door and I want to be able to prove without any doubt that I was in Glasgow that night with a few of the lads. Get me?'

'It'll be worth another couple of thousand.'

He shook his head, regretfully I thought.

'I stay out of trouble by not getting too involved. What's wrong with baby doll, here?'

'Her name's Miss Atkinson to you, Singer,' I said, smiling, although my heart was thumping away like a bass drum with the twitch.

'And mine's Mister Singer to you.' He spoke pleasantly enough, but his eyes were glittering again and his big fingers flexed.

'Why do you need anyone else?' Marie put in quickly, before he could start any trouble.

'I need someone to help me. All you'd have to do would be keep a watch while I concentrate on getting the safe open.

You'd have to warn me if anyone showed up.'

'Who's likely to show up?'

'No one if what Singer says is true.' I grinned at him and then wiped it off when he shifted forward a few inches in his chair, Rupert Bear gleaming as the light began to fade outside. Any more baiting and it would be me who started to fade, and I decided it was quitting time.

'Mr Singer says there won't be anyone, but you never know. Bannister could change his mind for once.'

'Are you sure this is going to be safe?' she said, frowning.

'Honey, nothing like this is ever safe. All we can do is take all the precautions we can think of. If we don't act like a couple of amateurs there shouldn't be any trouble.'

'The only trouble will be if it comes into your head to double cross me,' Singer said, rubbing his ear.

'I wouldn't dream of it,' I said, even

though an idea like that had been crawling around in my mind. He struck me as being too cocky for his own good, and from what he had told me I didn't reckon I was getting fair value for my five thousand. I wasn't going to argue now; if I argued at all it would be when I had those diamonds safe in my pocket.

'Just keep it in mind,' he said.

'If there is any danger, Bannister's the character it'll come from.'

And remembering how big he was I knew that if he heard us we'd have more problems than a snowball in a stove. I didn't tell Marie that. It might have frightened her so much that she'd never have come in with me at all.

'How are you going to open the safe?' she asked.

'There are keys,' Singer said. 'It would have been too dangerous to ask where they were, but you can hunt around until you find them.'

Eventually I persuaded her, and Singer

left. We settled it for a couple of nights ahead, when Marie had no engagements and when no one would be able to see that she was nervous. I spent the day waiting in a frenzy of impatience, and on the night I drove out to Bannister's place. Neither of us spoke much on the way. I stopped the car at the entrance to the drive, reversed and backed in, leaving it out of sight from the road but in a position where we could get it out in a hurry.

'Don't slam the doors as you get out,' I told her.

We made our way up the drive. The patch of oil that I'd let drip from Christie's car had gone, I noticed in the light from the torch. We went right round the building, pushing our way through tangled grass and bushes at the back, and eventually I found the open window I'd been hoping to see. It was hard to get at but it was just what we wanted, and even Marie brightened when she saw in. In a nearby shed I found a ladder. Five minutes later, we were in.

The house was dark. Its atmosphere oppressed me. We didn't say much as we hunted for the key, finding it eventually in a little compartment at the back of one of the desk drawers. All the time we were looking I could hear unnerving little creaks as the house settled in for the night, and once there was a faint scratching at the door which sent Marie whirling round in a flat panic, her breath coming in short little gasps, the torchlight dancing crazily.

'It's only a mouse,' I muttered. 'Keep that torch still so that no one outside can see it through the curtains.'

'Where's the safe?' she asked, looking at the keys I was dangling in my hand.

'This way.'

We left the small office and went through the hall into the room I'd blundered into on my earlier visit. The safe was in one corner of the room and I tried the keys one by one until it opened. Singer had been right. There weren't any problems, and for the first time I really began to feel that he'd earned his five thousand quid.

The safe was empty.

I dropped the torch on the floor. It clattered, but didn't go out. I could see Marie's face as a pale blur then I grabbed the torch again and flashed it into the safe. It wasn't as empty as I'd thought, but a bundle of papers, fifteen pounds in scruffy one pound notes and some loose change in a tin box were no substitute for the bag full of diamonds that I'd been expecting.

Marie's face was white and frightened, her lips pressed together. I grabbed her arm and swung her round to face me.

'Well?' I demanded. 'What smart trick is this? What have you cooked up together, you and Singer? Mr Singer.'

'There's nothing, Wayne,' she said, trying to break free and not managing it. 'Nothing at all. I thought—'

'You're like me, you thought wrong,' I snarled. 'When I get hold of Singer I'll break his neck. He won't be so interested in Rupert Bear when I've finished with him.'

'Wayne—'

'Where does he live?'

'Why?'

'We'll go round there now. I'll work him over until—'

'Wayne, could there be another safe?' she gasped out, trying not to show that I was hurting her arm where I was squeezing it.

'Another safe?' I said blankly. That hadn't occurred to me.

She nodded.

'I've never known Mr Singer be wrong before and there's no reason why he should be now.'

Her words hit me with the force of bullets.

'What do you mean, you've never known him wrong before? You haven't done this sort of thing in the past, have you?'

'Let's look for this safe,' she said sullenly. 'The sooner we can get out

59

of this creepy joint the better I'll like it.'

'Yeah,' I said thoughtfully. 'Me, too.'

We left the room, and Marie stayed downstairs where she could watch the drive while I had a look round upstairs. That was a nervy business because I'd no idea where Bannister actually slept and I could walk in on him any minute, but at last I found another office, complete with desk, filing cabinets and a tiny safe opened by an equally tiny key on the bunch I already had.

The diamonds were there, more than before, neatly parcelled up in their little leather bag and tucked away at the back. I grinned into the darkness, then teemed them out onto the desk, playing the torch on them and watching them glitter and sparkle. It made up for everything and I understood now why Bannister had been playing with them that day, just pushing them about the desk with no particular purpose in mind; it was a very satisfying feeling, watching all that money winking at you and knowing that you'd got your hands on it at last.

I could have stood there with them all night, but presently I remembered where I was, scooped them back into their bag and turned to go.

That was when I heard the noise.

I stood absolutely still. It was a quiet, slithering sound from the passage outside, and listening to it made the hairs on my neck spring to attention like so many soldiers. I moved carefully towards the door, though I would rather have jumped out of the window, and had I been on the ground floor I probably would have done. The sound went on. I paused at the door, switching off the torch and trying to still my breathing.

The door began to open very slowly.

I drew a breath and snatched at the handle, tearing it out of the grasp of whoever was coming in. At the same moment, I switched the torch back on and shone it into his face, hoping to blind him for a minute.

It was Bannister.

He yelled at me as I jumped forward but I had the advantage of surprise and I managed to get past him. My feet thudded on the carpet as I ran down the long passage, and I could tell that Bannister wasn't far behind me. In the darkness, it was hard to be sure where the passage ended and the stairs began, and I had cut the torch again so as not to give him too much help at seeing where I was. Just as I reached the top of the stairs he caught me. His fingers closed on my collar and I was pulled up so fast that I thought he'd cut my legs off.

'Dirty thief!' he hissed into my ear, spinning me round so that he could get a better look at me.

I fought, trying to get out of his grip, but it was hopeless. His fingers were like steel clamps, and from the expression on his face, which I could see dimly in the darkness, he was going to have a little revenge of his own before he called the cops.

If he called the cops. I remembered what Singer had said about the diamonds being used as a tax fraud; from the number of stones it was one hell of a big fraud and I went as cold as a fish on a slab as I realized what that could mean.

His fist came up at me. I ducked but the blow caught my shoulder. There was a lot of power behind it, but that didn't stop him sending up another one almost at once; as it whipped over my head I realized that he was off balance and I could twist free. My collar tore as I did so, but I wasn't worried about that.

We wrestled at the top of the stairs.

Suddenly, he stumbled. He gave a hoarse cry as he bounced away, tumbling over and over down the long flight of stairs, his head striking the treads from time to time. There was a thump like a bag of cement falling down a coal chute as he hit the bottom.

His cries stopped and at the same moment all the lights came on and a girl began to scream.

III

The first thought that came into my mind was that it must be something to do with Marie, but as my mind started to work properly again I realized that it was coming from behind me. I took a quick look. It was the girl who had let me in when I had called on Christie's business; maybe Singer had been wrong when he said there was only Bannister in the house, or maybe she was his fancy woman just staying for the night. I didn't know, but all she had on was a black nightdress which would have interested me some other time.

She was looking directly at me, but her eyes were blank with fear and I don't think she recognized me.

I pounded down the stairs.

Bannister was lying at the bottom. His

head was twisted right round and his lips were drawn back from his teeth, ready for another of those hoarse cries. Blood was trickling slowly from his left ear, making a puddle on the expensive carpet. He looked horrible. He was dead.

The girl screamed again. I ran past Bannister without stopping to take too close a look, only concerned about finding Marie and getting out. She came into the passage as I reached the front door.

'Don't stop!' I cried to her. 'Get out of the door fast.'

I was certain then that she'd broken into other places because she didn't waste any time asking for explanations. When we were outside and I grabbed her arm to pull her along faster she said:

'The diamonds. Have you got them?'

I nodded, too out of breath to speak. We reached the car without anyone coming after us. It started at the first touch and I rammed in the gears and spun the wheels on the loose gravel as I pulled away.

'What went wrong?' she asked when I'd put a couple of miles between us and the house and thought it safe to slow down a little.

'Bannister came in and caught me. There was a girl, too, the one who let me in that day I called.'

'Did she recognize you?'

'I don't know,' I said, shaking my head to try and clear it a little.

'You killed Bannister,' Marie said, and turned sideways so that she could look at me.

'He fell down the stairs. That's what killed him.'

'They'll say you pushed him.'

I was silent. I wanted to tell Marie that she was wrong and that it would be obvious that he'd fallen, but I knew that wasn't what the cops would think. Someone breaking into the house. Diamonds missing. Bannister catching the thief and being killed. That would be murder in their eyes and if that girl remembered who I was I would really be in the hot seat.

'They might not get the cops,' I said. 'If he was using those diamonds in a tax fraud they—'

Marie laughed, a harsh, cackling sound which showed that in spite of her apparent calm her nerves were pulled as taut as mine.

'No one need say anything about the diamonds, you jerk,' she said. 'You were just a thief after what you could get. When they catch you and you start talking about diamonds they'll wriggle out of it easily enough. Someone like Bannister will have got a lot of smart cookies round him to talk him out of things like that. Alive or dead.'

'What do you mean, when they catch me?' I snarled at her, swinging the car round a sharp bend. 'Wouldn't it be better to say if they get me?'

'They'll get you, Wayne,' she said with a sad little smile.

I slowed the car some more so that I

could reach into my pocket without so much danger of hitting anything.

'Here,' I said, taking out the leather bag, 'you'd better have these. If the cops come to see me I want to deny everything. I can't do that if they can find this stuff in the flat.'

She took the bag.

'He tore your collar,' she said.

'I know.'

'You'd better let me have that shirt as well. If they find that in your flat they won't need any diamonds because that's a clincher on its own. The tear will match the part that's still at Bannister's.'

I hadn't thought of that but my mind wasn't exactly clear and sharp. I drove to Marie's place as quickly as I could, and changed my shirt for an old one that was there.

'The best thing,' I said, tugging it over my head and buttoning it up fast, 'is for me to keep away from you for a couple of days, just so there can't be any slip up.

I'll phone you sometime tomorrow night. If Singer comes round you'll better tell him to cool it for a bit.'

'What shall I do if he won't wait?'

'He'll have to wait,' I yelled at her. 'Buy him a new Rupert book or something. That should keep him quiet for a day or two.'

She nodded, looking white faced and scared.

'You don't think the cops will come here, do you?'

'I don't know,' I said impatiently. 'I'm not going to tell them anything about you so they shouldn't get hold of your name. You haven't done anything else that they're after you for, have you?'

'Wayne—'

'Leave it,' I sneered. 'We'll talk about it later.'

I drove away. Everything depended on whether or not that girl had recognized me. I didn't think she had, but you could never tell. She had taken a good look at me and the cops would go into it with her pretty thoroughly; she might remember something then that she didn't remember now, if you see what I mean. They would call on Christie right away, who could be counted on to tell them who I was, and although it would take them a while to track their way through everything, in the end it would be just as Marie had said.

They'd come, all right.

And if I slipped up then it would be prison. I began to sweat again at the thought of what that would mean and by the time I reached my flat my hands were shaking so much that I could hardly drive properly.

I never meant to kill him. That's what every killer says when he's caught. In my case it happened to be true but that wouldn't stop the words from sounding as thin and pathetic in court as they did for everyone else, who didn't mean them. I might even get a couple of extra years for my cheek in expecting people to believe anything as stupid as that. I was in a jam, and it wasn't something I was going to be able to talk my way out of easily.

Marie rang me up the following afternoon, but there was nothing else I could tell her. In a way that was good, because I reckoned that if the cops were coming I might have heard something from them by now. There'd been a brief item in the morning papers, but no mention of the diamonds.

It was the evening paper which gave me the shock.

On the front page. A Photofit picture of me, constructed from the girl's description. She hadn't remembered seeing me before and the picture wasn't a very good one, but it was near enough for me to be able to imagine people I knew commenting on it. I began to sweat again and my fears, which had faded slightly, came back, stronger than before.

I hardly slept that night. Every few minutes I woke up, imagining that I'd heard the stolid tread and the ring at the bell which would herald the arrival of the cops. They could come any time, of course, not only during the day; as soon as they thought they'd nailed me, they'd be here.

I ate nothing for breakfast. My face looked grey and ugly and I knew that if I didn't do something they'd only have to look at me to see that something was wrong, and know that they'd come to the right place. I tried phoning Marie but there was no answer and I guessed that she'd be out at work somewhere, trying to carry on as normal and probably making a better job of it than I was doing.

But then, she hadn't killed Bannister. Even if the cops did come they weren't going to get her for much.

Unless she'd done something on her own that they could pick her up for.

That interested me and I would have liked to have gone into it further with her. When this scare was over, if I was still free,

I was going to, but in the meantime I had all day to think about it. Had it been her idea or mine to take the jewels? It was mine, there was no getting away from that, but if she hadn't had the contacts we would have had to give up the plan. She was at least as much to blame as me, but the law wouldn't see it that way.

The law didn't even know she'd been there because that girl hadn't seen her.

I sat in my room all day again, and when the bell eventually rang, at tea time, it was more of a relief than anything else. I went to the door, actually managing to smile as I opened it. And then the smile froze on my face. The caller wasn't a cop.

It was Maurice Longford.

IV

'Well?' I asked. I tried to speak normally, but there was a cold fear inside me much worse than anything the police could have

73

inspired as I tried to work out what he could want.

'Can I have a minute or two?' he said.

I opened the door wider and stepped aside to give him room to mince in. As he did so, he took off his silk scarf and wrapped it into a small bundle which he dropped into his pocket.

'A seat?'

He chose the armchair. I closed the door and stood by the empty grate, waiting for him to speak. My manner didn't seem to worry him at all, and he leaned back comfortably with the drink I gave him. He looked at it a little sneeringly, as if it wasn't quite what he was used to, but I couldn't have cared less about that. He could think himself lucky not to have been given a glass of poison; I hated him for the way I reckoned he'd dragged Marie down, and I didn't care whether he knew it or not.

'What do you want?' I demanded.

He set the glass down and gave me a

tiny smile which was probably considered frightfully smart in the set he moved with.

'Where's Marie?' he asked bluntly.

'What do you mean, where is she?'

'Let me put it another way,' he said, taking up the glass again and sipping daintily. 'If you had to go and find her now, where would you go?'

'Her flat.' Little tremors of alarm were having a fine time climbing up my spine and then sliding down again, but I didn't let him see any of that.

He waved his arm impatiently.

'She's closed up her flat. You've been going around with her for long enough. You must know something about that.'

'Closed it up?'

'Two days ago.'

'But she rang me up yesterday,' I said stupidly. 'She didn't say anything about it then.'

He smirked at me.

'That's tough, old boy. Not as well in

with her as you thought, eh? The only trouble so far as I'm concerned is that she agreed to do some very important photos for me this morning. For some special clients, you know.'

I didn't care about him or his lousy photos. I had a date with her myself, and I had an even more interesting date with the twenty thousand pounds worth of diamonds that she was holding for me. I'd killed a man to get them, and right now I wanted them even more than I wanted her.

Longford was still smirking at me.

I picked him out of the chair by his collar, twisting it tightly so that his plucking hands couldn't pull it away from his throat.

'What have you done with her?' I snarled. 'Is this some smart trick of yours?'

He didn't speak. Probably that was because there wasn't enough space in his throat to let the words pass. To give him a better chance I dropped him back into the chair where he bounced up and down gently on the springs, glaring at me, his face purple.

'I can assure you that there's no trick,' he said hoarsely. 'Why should there be?'

'So that you can get hold of—' I stopped, appalled at how easily I could have given myself away.

He was looking at me sharply.

'Get hold of what?' he asked.

'Marie,' I said weakly. 'You were doing fine until I came along. Maybe this is something you've cooked up because you don't want any competition.'

'I don't have to worry about competition from people like you,' he said carefully. 'I can give Marie more in a week than you can give her in a year. But for me, she wouldn't be anywhere.'

I picked him up again then. The purple of his face seemed to blur at the edges until I was seeing everything through a purple mist. I knew that I'd hit something and I guessed from the yell that it was

77

Longford. When I saw him clearly again he was rubbing his face and I was at the other side of the room.

'Get out,' I said. 'If I ever see you again I'll twist your head right off your neck.'

That reminded me of Bannister and I started shivering. I knew Longford was looking at me queerly but when I took a step towards him he didn't hang around. He whipped his scarf out of his pocket and ran.

His drink was still by the chair, where he had left it. I stood and looked at it for a few seconds then I took careful and deliberate aim and kicked it as hard as I could. It spun across the room, smashing against the wall. The whisky trickled down the wallpaper and made a small pool on the carpet.

I didn't care.

Maybe Marie had moved out for some other reason, and she intended to give me a call telling me where she was living now. That was always a hope, but somehow I knew that I was never going to see her or the diamonds again, and that the best I could hope for was that the cops wouldn't come bothering me. Worse was the fact that she still had the torn shirt which would match up with the piece that the police had taken from between Bannister's fingers. That was the final evidence, and that could be used against me years later, if it was ever produced.

A fine thing for Marie and her mates to have.

Singer was one of her mates.

Was he in on this double cross, or was I likely to find him panting at the door, asking for the diamonds so that he could sell them and pocket his share of the money. Marie's gone and taken them with her, I would tell him, while his luminous Rupert Bear glared at me. There was about as much chance of getting him to believe that as there was of bringing Bannister back to life. If he wasn't in with her there was little chance for me. With him and the cops on my tail it wouldn't be long before one of them got me.

And much as I dreaded jail I'd rather have been caught by the cops.

Just to make sure that Longford wasn't pulling some stunt of his own I rang Marie's number several times in the course of the evening, and got no answer. The next day I actually went round, and a neighbour confirmed everything that Longford had said. While we were talking I noticed that she was staring hard at me, and it was that more than anything else which brought home to me the danger I was in.

There'd been nothing yet from the cops or Singer, but that didn't mean things were going to stay that way. In addition, I had no money and little chance of getting any. I didn't kid myself that I'd committed the greatest crime of the century, and I reckoned that outside London very little would have been heard of it; certainly, I didn't think the police would have bothered to circulate the Photofit picture say in the

North, though you could never tell.

So that there was where I wanted to go. I didn't know what I was going to do when I got there, nor was I worried too much; all I wanted to do at that stage was get out of the way of the cops and Singer, and I reckoned that was the best place to do it.

The only trouble was that I didn't have any money. I wasn't actually flat broke but there wasn't a lot in it and by the time I'd got there and found a flat I wouldn't have much left. Everything came back to the old problem. If I had a few hundred pounds I wouldn't be worrying, but then, if I'd had money in the first place Bannister would probably have still been alive, and I wouldn't have been in a mess.

And at least the cops were keeping away. To my way of thinking if anyone was going to tell them about me, or recognize that picture and pass on the information, they would have done it by now. If I waited where I was until my money was as low as I dared let it go, and didn't draw attention to myself, there was a hope that the whole scare would soon die down and the danger, while it wouldn't be over, would be nowhere near as great as it was now.

So I settled into a new routine, only going out when I had to, seeing no one and having no callers. By the end of the third day I thought I was going to go mad, but at least it was giving everyone a chance to forget that Wayne Edwards existed, and it was giving me a chance to sort out what I was going to do afterwards, when I had to go out and get some more money.

Maybe you're thinking that was a tame way of going about things after I'd been double-crossed, to the tune of thirty thousand pounds, and I'd be inclined to go along with you. The trouble was that I didn't want to draw too much attention to myself, nor could I see how to go about finding the girl. The problem was to guess where she was in the whole of London, with no clues and no one to help me; she was in my mind a lot during those three days, but I couldn't see any solution to the problem or any way of getting my share of the diamonds.

The mood I was in by then I'd have taken the lot and left her and Singer without a penny. He was another danger that I hadn't forgotten, though I didn't really expect him to come. It was obvious to me now that he'd been working with her from the start, and he'd only led me along to save having to do any of the heavy work for himself.

I was a mug, there was no doubt about it, and possibly Christie had been right when he had advised me, years ago it seemed, to have nothing to do with Marie Atkinson but to leave her to Longford.

That was all I thought about for three days.

After that, I had plenty to think about,

because a girl called Sandra Howell came to see me.

She was the girl who'd been at Bannister's on the night of the murder.

Chapter Three

I recognized her as soon as I opened the door. She was wearing a smart, dark green suede coat and her hair was done differently from how it had been the last time I'd seen her, but there was no mistaking her. If I had been in any doubt, the way she looked at me, first with a faint smile on her face, then pursing her lips as if she'd known that she'd been right all along, would have given me the clue. She was confident, I had to give her that; for her, seeing me at the door was only confirmation of what she already knew.

'What do you want?' I demanded, hardly recognizing the hoarse croak as my own voice.

'Can I come in?'

Now it was my turn to smile, though

there was nothing funny about the thoughts which were seething in my mind.

'What happens if I say you can't?' I asked.

'I'll leave that to your imagination,' she said sweetly, not put out at all.

It didn't take much imagination to realize what she was getting at, and I opened the door wider to let her step into the flat, then slammed it as a way of venting my feelings on something that couldn't hit back.

'Temper,' she said, as I sat down.

'Just get on with what you've come to say and never mind the fancy remarks,' I told her.

'Don't you even offer a girl a drink when she comes to see you?'

I pressed my lips together then went over to the cupboard where I kept what drinks I could afford. Having her drink the stuff didn't help my mood any, but there was no point in arguing uselessly with her.

When I looked more closely at her she didn't look as smart as she had done the first time I'd seen her, when I'd pushed my way past her to Bannister's room, nor as sexy as she had done in that nightie on the day I'd killed him. There were signs of strain at the corners of her mouth and her eyes were puffy, with dark circles beneath them. Whether Bannister's death had broken her up, whether the cops had been at her, or whether there was some other reason, I didn't know. I guessed that I soon would, but it was up to her to make the play.

She balanced her drink on the arm of the chair, unfastened her coat and smoothed her blue woollen dress over her legs. She was in no hurry. Eventually she'd get round to it. I watched her, then looked towards the window; it was a poor effort to seem unconcerned at the sight of her, but it was the best I could do.

'You are Wayne Edwards, aren't you?' she asked.

Somehow, although she was here, I hadn't been expecting her to know my name, and it gave me quite a jolt to hear her trot it out like that.

'What if I am?'

'I only want to make sure. I'm Sandra Howell.'

'So now we know each other, where does that get us?' I sneered. 'And what are you doing here. How did you find out where I lived?'

'It wasn't hard,' she said, leaning back and smiling at me again. There was a faint undercurrent of tension in her manner, but if she was at all nervous of being with a killer she hid it well. 'The worst part was when I was talking to the police and trying to convince them I hadn't seen you properly.'

'You gave them a fair description of me.'

'I had to give them something,' she said with a shrug. 'I couldn't pretend to be a complete fool because they know very well that Charles would never have employed a fool as his secretary.'

'Charles being the late Bannister, of course?'

'That's right. Besides, the cops make it easy for you with those Photofit things. All you do is pick out a nose, a mouth, ears and so on that match the ones you saw. Unless you're deliberately trying to mislead them you can't go far wrong.'

'Were you trying to fool them?'

'I'd have liked to but I didn't dare go too far in case they picked you up and wondered why my description was so far out. As it was, I got away with it.'

'So have I.'

'Up to now,' she said. 'You didn't mean to kill Charles did you?'

'It was an accident,' I told her wearily, tired of trying to convince myself that was how it had been without starting on an outsider. 'If he hadn't come interfering with me he'd be alive today. You still haven't told me how you got here.'

'When I first saw you that night I didn't remember who you were,' she said. 'It was while I was waiting for the police to finish their routine and get round to asking me questions that I realized you were the person who'd come from Christie's advertising agency and barged into Charles's study.'

'Did he say anything about that?' I interrupted.

'He wasn't bothered,' she said casually. 'Things like that didn't worry him much.'

'And what did you do then?'

'After I'd remembered who you were?' She smiled. 'I saw the possibilities of it, kept quiet to the cops and then went to get your address from Christie's. It wasn't difficult.'

I really started to sweat then. Whatever the little fool wanted here, if she'd been blurting things out to Christie it could be just the thing he needed to jog his memory. I stared at her and she smiled back at me.

'Did you see Alf Christie himself?' I demanded.

'No. There was a young lad in the office.

He was very helpful. He said that he didn't know you but he looked things up in the records and so on and told me everything I wanted to know.'

'He must have replaced me,' I said. 'All right, you're here and you haven't told the cops about me. Why? What do you want?'

'I should have thought that was obvious. I want my share of the diamonds. Stealing them was something that I'd been thinking about for months, ever since I knew that he had them in the house. I'd have done it, too, except that I'd have been the obvious suspect and even if I got them I didn't know any easy way of turning them into money.'

I gave her a jeering grin.

'I haven't got any diamonds,' I said. 'You might have seen that there was a girl with me. After the killing I gave her the diamonds to look after in case you gave my name to the cops and they came to see me. She's gone. The diamonds have gone with her.'

I never thought that I'd have got any enjoyment out of the fact that Marie had skipped. I did then, but not for long, because I could see that Sandra didn't believe a word I'd said. That worried me; if she got it into her head that I was spinning her a line there was no telling what she might do to persuade me to see things her way.

'You can't really think—'

'It's the truth, Sandra, take it or leave it. Marie Atkinson is the girl's name. You try and find her if you want to but I don't think you'll manage it. Even if you do, there won't be much chance of getting the diamonds out of her.'

'Look,' she said, 'those diamonds were worth a little over thirty thousand pounds. What you're asking me to believe is that you went to all that trouble to get them, killed a man for them, and then let her walk off with them? It doesn't work, Wayne.'

'It's the score.'

'It's so much like a put-up job that it stinks. Remember I could get you in prison for years and years if I went to the cops.'

'Go to who the hell you like,' I snarled, 'but it won't change anything. I trusted Marie and when I thought that the cops might search my flat I gave them to her so that they wouldn't find them. When I went round to see her a couple of days afterwards, she'd gone.'

I spoke very slowly, as if I were trying to explain something to a child, but I could see that it wasn't working. It was like trying to convince a South Sea Islander that there aren't really little men and women inside the television set.

'What are you doing about her?' she asked. 'You can't sit back like a big slob and not do a thing.'

After three days of solid thinking I had my own ideas on that, but I wasn't going to pass them on to this little chiseller.

'Let's look at it another way,' I said.

'Suppose I tell you to get lost. What will you do then?'

She looked at me for a minute or two, sipping her drink, then reached down to her bag, snapped it open and took out a pack of cigarettes. She offered me one but I waved it aside. When she had lit her own, her hand trembling slightly and making the match flame scutter about, she leaned back again and flicked the match casually into the fireplace.

'I'll go back to the cops,' she said, 'and tell them I've remembered one or two other things about you. They'll take my word for it and you can bet that they'll be round here before morning.'

'And if I tell them that you came here trying to blackmail me, and only remembered these things after I'd refused to pay, where do you stand then?'

'They wouldn't take a scrap of notice of you,' she said, blowing a cloud of smoke towards the ceiling. 'You're a thief, a killer, and they'd think that you were raving anything that came into your head, simply because I'd given them the tip-off about you.'

I leered at her.

'You've hit it right on the head, baby,' I said, hunching forward in my chair so as to get nearer to her. 'I'm a killer. You've just said so. What's to stop me from killing you now, and stopping your little yapping mouth for good? You're the only one who can finger me, don't forget.'

'My boyfriend knows I'm coming here,' she said, her voice unsteady. 'I'm supposed to be meeting him later. If I don't show up he'll tell the police about you and they'll come here before they do anything else. One look at you will be enough to tell them who you are.'

'But that won't help you.' I was still leering. 'You'll be rotting in the Thames by then.'

'It'll help me now,' she said, 'because if you were thinking of killing me the thought of the danger it'll put you in should stop you.'

'It should do, baby, but will it?'

She swallowed. What I couldn't tell her was that she was right. The other thing that she didn't know was that even without any threat like that I could never have brought myself to clamp my fingers round her lovely little throat and squeeze the life out of her. Had I done so I would probably have saved myself a lot of trouble, but apart from the risk it simply wasn't in me to kill her deliberately, like that, at a snap of the fingers so to speak.

Singer, if he came after me, yes. Even Marie, if I ever met her again. But not this girl, right here in my flat.

I shrugged.

'What happens now? I say I haven't got any diamonds and you say I have. What do you intend to do about it?'

'I want them,' she said, her voice calmer now that we were off the subject of whether or not I was going to kill her.

'You can't have them, Sandra honey, because I haven't got them. If I had I don't reckon you'd rate for any share in the handout.'

That was the wrong thing to say. I knew that as soon as the glint slid into her eyes. Up to now they had been more or less normal but when I looked at her after that I got quite a shock. It was like looking through a hole in a fence and finding another pair of eyes looking back at you.

'You would give me a share,' she said harshly. 'You'd have no choice because you can't afford to have me go to the police. I want a half share and you'd better make up your mind now that I'm going to have it.'

'There isn't a half share to give you!' I was getting desperate now. I had to convince her. If I couldn't things would fall apart before morning and there wouldn't be a thing I could do about it.

'You'll have to find this girl, what's her

name, Marie,' she said bluntly. 'That's if you really have let her disappear with them.'

'I wouldn't know where to start looking. Why do you think I'm still sitting here?'

'You'd better get to know. If you can't find her I don't imagine anyone else would be able to. If she helped you steal them you must know her pretty well.'

'I do know her well,' I said patiently, 'but now she's gone into hiding it doesn't help me find her, does it? She won't go to any of the places that I can think of because she'll be able to guess that I could find her there. She's going to keep away from everywhere she usually goes to. For all I know she could have left London.'

I grinned at her again. The strange glint was still in her eyes and I began to think that the thought of the power she had over me, and the money she'd worked out it would bring her, had started to turn her brain. If someone had walked through the door and told me she was mad it wouldn't have surprised me in the least, and from the cold way in which she was talking I knew that she would do anything she threatened she would.

She was as safe as a basket of cobras with the lid off. I ought to have killed her there and then, but it just wasn't in me.

She said: 'I'll be fair with you. I'll give you a couple of days then I'll come back, and you'd better have some money for me. I don't care how much it is as long as it's more than a thousand pounds. I'm going to leave a letter with my boyfriend, too, so that if anything happens to me there'll be no doubt who's to blame.'

I nodded, not bothering to speak. There was nothing worth saying by then.

She tossed the rest of her drink down her throat, placed the empty glass neatly in the middle of the table, and went to the door.

'You'd better find your girlfriend, Wayne, and be quick about it,' she said, opened the door and went out.

I shivered as I closed it after her. She was like me, in that she'd do anything for money; the only problem was that I hadn't got any and she thought I had.

I spent the rest of the evening sitting in a chair, trying to work things out. Even if I could have raised a thousand pounds over the next couple of days it would have been stupid to have given it to her; apart from being more or less an admission that I had money and was willing to be blackmailed, it would never have stopped there. I might have been a mug over Marie but I wasn't as big a sucker as all that. Another thousand would have followed, then another and another and another. That's how it would have gone on, and always the threat of the visit to the cops if I failed to meet the payments, or the letter she'd written naming me if anything happened to her.

If she was killed by a truck on her way to the shops tomorrow morning, this boyfriend of hers would run to the cops and say I'd arranged it.

There was no other course open to me. I'd have to clear out, change my address and work out what to do next.

Not that there was much choice open to me about that. I could either go under, staying as penniless as I was now, get another job and be no better off than I had been before the murder, or I could do as Sandra had suggested and try to find Marie. I'd left it late to start anything like that, but that might have its advantages in that by now she'd think that I wasn't coming after her. It worked two ways, and if I asked round for long enough I was sure to come up with some trace of her.

That was what I decided, anyway. Whether it worked or not, it was better than staying here to be fleeced by Sandra Howell.

As soon as I'd decided that I stood up. It was late, but not so late that I couldn't book into a hotel that same night. I hadn't many things, and they fitted easily into a battered old suitcase I used to take on holiday with me. I didn't care which hotel I went to so long as it was somewhere quiet and obscure, a place where I could lose myself while I worked to find Marie and the diamonds.

I didn't lose myself quickly enough. As I glanced out of the window before leaving I saw Singer turning in at the street door.

II

He hadn't seen me, I was sure of that. All I'd done was look quickly out of the window, and even if he'd spotted the movement he had no way of knowing which was my window because he'd never been here before. I was still standing at the side of the room as he disappeared from view into the entrance hall; the sight of him seemed to have frozen my mind and limbs, and I could neither move nor think of any plan.

At any other time, by talking fast enough

and not getting in the way of those King Kong arms I might have made a job of convincing him that I was as much in the dark as he was himself, but not now. Not with my case packed, and everything ready for me to flit into the night. The minute he saw that he would know that all he'd been thinking about me had been right, and he'd deal with it in his own simple way.

In any event, even if I convinced him that I'd no diamonds and wasn't trying to double cross him, it wouldn't do me any good; like Sandra Howell he'd know that I'd killed Bannister, and I imagined that his ideas on what to do with that piece of information would be much the same as hers. Perhaps that was what he was really after and why he'd come here, but I didn't intend staying to find out. Things were in a mess, but if I could once get my hands on Marie again I knew that I could sort them out and put my affairs into something like normal order.

Quietly, I opened the door. Singer would

be on his way up the stairs by now, and it would take him another half minute or so to reach my door. I listened. At first there was nothing, then I heard the faint clumping of his feet, drawing nearer with every step.

I had to get out of the building, without using the stairs. Put like that it sounded simple, and as my mind started to work again I realized that it was.

Across from my flat and at the other end of the passage from the stairs was an empty room. It was an odd one out, a room that they hadn't been able to fit into any flat when the house had been converted, and as far as I knew it was used as some kind of store room; the door was locked, of course, but it only had the same sort of not too brilliant fastening as my own door, easy enough to open with the blade of a penknife or a strip of celluloid. I'd used that method of breaking into the flat on a couple of occasions when I'd forgotten my key, and I knew that the transparent case I put my driving licence in would be ideal.

Before Singer had climbed another two stairs I'd humped my case across the passage, shut my own door and started work on the lock. I got it open just as he reached the top of the stairs, only just in time. In my hurry to get into the other room I almost fell over the case, which banged against the door with a noise which I was sure he must have heard and which had me panicking even more until I managed to get a hold on myself again.

There was a glimpse of a brightly coloured shirt and trousers with Singer inside them turning into the passage, then I had the door shut and was leaning on it, waiting for my heart to stop thumping and my breathing to return to normal.

The sound of Singer's footsteps stopped and there was a pause of a couple of seconds before I heard him hammering on my door. I wondered how he'd got my address. Because I hadn't been living there for long enough the phone was still under the name of the previous occupant, so looking me up in the book wouldn't have done any good. The only other way I could think of was that Marie had given it to him and if that was so it meant that she wanted to fix me properly and must have fed him the yarn that I'd double crossed both of them.

The thought of how she'd taken me for a sucker didn't do me much good, and neither would standing there while Singer was only a few yards away.

This room was dusty and dismal, with no light bulb in the socket, no carpet on the floor and no curtains at the grimy window. Stacked against the wall were a couple of old packing cases and a two foot length of lead piping. Thrown in a corner was a cheap, single bar electric fire, bent as if someone had trodden on it.

I shuddered, then crossed to the window and smeared some of the filth away with my hand so that I could see out. As I'd hoped, it gave onto what had been the back yard of the original house. No one used it much now, and apart from three dustbins and an outbuilding there was nothing in it. Across from where I was standing were the yards and backs of other houses, some with lighted windows, but I didn't bother about them; it was the outbuilding which interested me.

Cautiously, I tested the window. With some encouragement it slid upwards and I felt the coolness of the night air blowing in on my face. Picking up the case I hefted it onto the sill, then leaned out with it, as far as I could, and let it drop onto the flat roof of the outbuilding. It made a slight noise as it landed, then fell on its side and slid so near to the edge that I thought it was going to fall into the yard.

It stopped.

Now it was my turn.

Singer was still beating on my door. I could hear him clearly, and he sounded like a starving man trying to get into a cafe that was closed; if I'd needed any spurring on to climb out of the window, that would have provided it. Pretty soon, when he got no answer, I guessed that he'd break in and confirm that I'd left; what he'd do then I'd no idea, nor did it worry me as I wouldn't be around to see it.

I scrambled onto the window sill, then squeezed onto the cracked ledge outside. I didn't want to drop too heavily onto the roof, not only because it might make more noise than I'd like but because I was heavier than the suitcase and I didn't want to risk going right through. The drop from the ledge was further down than I'd thought, but by clambering around like a monkey until I was hanging with my fingertips just maintaining their hold I could touch the roof with my toes. I lowered myself gently, banged the dirt off my hands and then turned to drop into the yard.

A face was watching me.

My heart lurched as I saw it, pressed against the glass of the window of a house across the alley. Even after I'd realized what it was, and when it must have seen that I was watching it, it didn't move but continued to stare unblinkingly, the skin whitened by the pressure against the glass, the mouth set in a thin and unmoving straight line.

My heart pounded. Sweat started out on my brow. There was something horrible and malignant about that face, even though it didn't seem worried by the fact that I'd just climbed out of a window. I turned my back on it but I could still seem to see it floating in the semi darkness in front of my eyes. When I whipped round, trying to surprise it, it was still there, staring.

A woman, obviously with nothing better to do than watch all that went on. Provided she didn't take it into her head to tell anyone official what she'd seen, I didn't care. Picking up the suitcase I went right to the edge of the roof and looked into the yard.

There seemed no reason why I shouldn't drop down as easily as I'd done from the window. The drop was longer, but nothing to worry about, and after a moment I let go of the case. Again, I'd leaned as far over the edge as I'd dared, but I still thought that it was going to burst open when it hit the ground. It didn't, and neither did I when I followed it over, landing softly near one of the dustbins.

The face was still watching, I knew, although that wall of the yard stopped me from seeing it now.

The back gate was only latched. I opened it. There was a faint creaking whine from the hinges, but nothing to connect me with it in Singer's mind; as far as he knew, I could have gone any time in the past few days, and it wouldn't occur to him that I was only escaping now because I'd been lucky enough to see him.

Another thing I was thankful for was that

when I'd last parked the car it had had to be a few streets away because there'd been no room anywhere nearer. It meant that I could get into it now without attracting Singer's attention.

Throwing my suitcase onto the back seat I started the engine and pulled away.

Half an hour later I was booking in at a hotel.

III

It was a crummy place, not the sort of hotel you'd have found me anywhere near if I'd had the choice, but I didn't and I had to make the best of it. Any of the big, swank places, assuming that I could have afforded them, would have been risky because the cops were more likely to check with them to see if I was there. They wouldn't really be expecting me to go to a hotel, but checking them was part of the routine when they were looking for anyone; what I was hoping was that they'd have reasoned to themselves that no one with thirty thousand pounds worth of diamonds in his sock would stay in a tiny, beat up joint like this one.

It wasn't the kind of hotel that runs to any parking spaces of its own, but I found a croft not far away where a row of houses had been knocked down, and I left it there. I walked back to the hotel, humped my suitcase up the three, worn steps and pushed open the swing doors.

The paint was faded and starting to flake off, one of the glass panels was cracked and the handle on the lobby door went round three times before the lock caught and the door opened. Because of all this the Queen Victoria monograms just inside the hall looked even quainter and more old-fashioned than they needed to, adding to the sad and forlorn air that was hanging over everything.

The clerk at the desk looked up sharply when he heard me come in. He was reading a magazine with a nude on the cover that reminded me of Marie and Longford, and from the state of his face he hadn't been expecting anyone else that night. He crumpled the comic under the desk swiftly, and hitched up a smile from somewhere.

'You're very lucky, sir,' he said. 'I was just thinking about locking up for the night. Don't get many people at this time, and I like to close the doors and put my feet up for a while.' He winked. 'You know how it is?'

'I know how it is,' I agreed. 'Got any rooms?'

It was a stupid question; a dump like that always has rooms available.

He was nodding, fumbling under the counter again. He brought a big heavy book out, flipped it open and pushed it towards me. A pen was tied with string to a nail on his side of the desk and I was just about to sign my name with it when I realized with a shock that if Sandra Howell did go to the cops when she discovered I'd scarpered she'd be able to tell them who I was.

I broke out into a sweat, while the joker behind the desk looked at me curiously. The pen was actually touching the page by this time, and I scribbled the only false name that I could think of. Edward Wayne. I made up an address in Manchester, a city I've never set foot in, and pushed the book back to him.

He glanced at it. He must have been waiting for something to liven up the evening.

'No relation to John Wayne, eh, sir?' he asked, his crusty old face breaking into a grin.

'Just give me the key,' I said.

He reached behind him, took down a key from a pegboard and held it in his hand.

'The reason I asked was that I've a cousin called Wayne and he always used to be asked that question when he went to a hotel. It's old hat now, but I've always wanted to say it to someone.'

I leaned over the desk. I got so close to him that I could smell the whisky on his breath and see the edge of the comic peeping out from under the desk.

'Your cousin must have stayed at some funny hotels,' I snarled. 'Now just give me the key. I'm tired and all I want to do is go to bed. I don't want to listen to any smart cracks from you about my name.'

Anyone would have thought that I'd fired a machine gun burst around him. He almost flung the key at me in his eagerness to please, and he'd still not finished babbling his apologies by the time I had my case halfway to the steep flight of stairs.

'Do you want me to take it up for you, sir?' he shouted after me.

Something about the expression on my face when I looked back at him must have given him his answer, because he never came out from behind his desk.

I knew that I wasn't doing too well,

but in my state you wouldn't have done either. Within the last few hours I'd been threatened with exposure to the cops by a girl who'd actually seen me kill Bannister, blackmailed for thousands of pounds that I hadn't got, and been chased by a character who was as big as a truck, liked Rupert Bear and thought I was chiselling him out of five thousand quid.

The false name business had been about all I could take, and I didn't want to talk about it, much less listen to jokes, each one of which impressed the name more firmly into his mind, so that he'd remember it at once if anyone ever asked him. There was no reason to think that he'd be cute enough to turn it round into Wayne Edwards, of course, but if the cops showed him a picture of me and pressed him hard enough he might mention it in passing, just to get rid of them.

All I wanted to do now was sleep, forget what had happened for a few hours, and then lie in bed in the morning and think about how I was going to find Marie and what I was going to do to her when I did get her.

It was with pleasant thoughts about that in my mind that I fell asleep on the hard, creaking bed.

When I awoke I saw from my watch that it was quarter to seven. There were no sounds of anyone moving about the hotel, although it was fairly light outside, and I took a better look at the room than I'd been inclined to the night before.

It was the sort of room I'd expect in a place like that. A cracked washbasin, a wardrobe and dressing table were the only items of furniture in it. The wardrobe and dressing table were nothing to shout about, either; they looked as though the owner had gone round to the nearest junk shop and picked them up as a job lot, though the grey carpet was surprisingly new and thick, out of place in a hotel like this.

Getting out of bed, I went over to the window. It looked out onto a small yard, and though there were no outbuildings near enough to reach easily there was a drainpipe not far away which I might be able to climb down and reach a glass-roofed shed that was built onto the back of the hotel.

It wasn't ideal, but if the alternative was being caught by the cops I'd be able to get away fast enough by that route.

After I'd dressed and shaved I sat down on the edge of the bed to take stock of the situation. On the face of it, it was pretty bad, but when I went into it more deeply things weren't as hopeless as they'd looked the night before.

Sandra Howell knew who I was, if I didn't pay her she was going to give my name to the cops, and in addition to all that, Singer was looking for me.

That was the bad news.

The good news was that nothing would happen today, tomorrow or the next day, with any luck. By then, Sandra Howell would have realized that I wasn't coming back, and judging by the state she'd been in when I'd seen her she'd go straight to the cops. If they took her seriously, which they'd be bound to, considering she'd worked for Bannister, they'd have my name, but they still wouldn't have found me.

And by then I'd have had three days to look for Marie.

The more I thought about that, the more I realized I should have gone after her before this. What I think must have happened was that the shock of having killed Bannister and then hearing of how Marie had double crossed me had stopped my brain from working properly. Normally, I wouldn't have merely sat back like that and done nothing, and to me now it was incredible that I had.

A frozen mind was the only explanation for it. Well, my brain was working fine now, and as soon as I'd had breakfast I was going to make a start.

The meal wasn't as bad as I'd thought

it would be. The other people staying in the hotel didn't take any notice of me as I went into the dining room, dark and gloomy with carved panelling on the walls, a heavily ornamented plaster ceiling and two elaborate lamps, one at each end, which looked good but which were too dirty to give off much light.

Not that there were many other people. Two men who looked like not very successful commercial travellers, a middle aged character sitting so upright that he must have been pensioned off from the Army, and three elderly ladies who laughed and cackled their way through the meal like elderly ladies always do.

At first they made the room seem homely but after a time it began to grate on my already over-exposed nerves. Sitting there voluntarily was like rubbing a cube of sugar across a freshly broken tooth, just to see if it hurts. By the time I was drinking the watery coffee which I hadn't asked for but which had been dumped on the table, I'd had enough of them. It was a pity, because it looked as if they lived there full time. But I wasn't going to move out. For all that it was so rough it was exactly the kind of place I was looking for, where the owner wouldn't invite police attention because he probably had a few happy rackets of his own going and didn't want to worry his contacts.

The sun was shining when I got outside. The weather hadn't been too good for the past couple of days but now the bits of sky that I could see between the tall buildings were cloudless, and it was warm enough to go without coat.

I hadn't much idea what I was going to do, but the logical place to make a start was Marie's flat. It felt like old times as I drove up and left my car in the spot I'd always used. The building was quiet at this time of day, and when I knocked on Marie's door the sound was very loud, like I was beating a drum. It didn't get the door open, though, and after a minute or two I bent down and had a look at the lock.

That was a surprise. It wasn't the lock that had always been on when I'd been coming here, but a brand new one, the wood bare around it, as if someone had smashed the door open, and the lock had been replaced later.

Singer was the man who came to mind. That was interesting, because it meant that Marie must be double crossing him too; I wondered if it had been him or some other of her crooked friends, and what they'd found inside. Whatever had happened there wasn't much point in trying to get in myself, and I straightened up and turned away. As a last resort I knocked on the doors round about, trying to get more information, but I got no answers from any of them and had to give up.

There was nothing for me here.

The only other thing I could think of to do was try the model agencies and photographers. It wasn't a very hopeful way of finding her, because now that she had the diamonds there was no reason for her to continue as a model, but it was better than nothing.

It didn't get me anywhere at all.

For a start, I didn't realize that there were so many of them, big places that probably wouldn't have told me anything even if they knew the answer, medium sized places jealous of the bigger ones and so anxious to keep a good reputation that they were just as wary, and one-man places like Christie's advertising agency who were more worried about whether or not I was from the cops than anything else.

I made a list of them from the Yellow Pages book and tried them one after the other, calling in person because it was so easy for them to fob off someone who was on the phone. When I hadn't got anywhere after the first half dozen except up a lot of stairs and along miles of passages in old office buildings I felt like giving up; the thing that pushed me on was the thought that it would take her a week or two to get a worthwhile price for the diamonds, and knowing Marie she would have to get money from somewhere during that time.

I knew that she had no savings. The only thing she could do was work, and she'd have to do that through one of the Agencies. So I'd thought, anyway, but things didn't seem to be coming out that way.

'I'm sorry, sir,' coldly efficient girls in the bigger Agencies and photographers told me. 'We can't give details like that to members of the public.'

Back down the stairs and into the street. Try one of the smaller places next. There's one handy and they might not be as stuffy.

'Can't tell you things like that,' a bloke with slicked down hair and a hooked nose tells me. 'Wouldn't do if we passed on our girls' addresses to everyone who asked, you can see that, can't you?'

'But I know Marie Atkinson. I'm a

friend of hers. I've already said that.'

'Then if you're all that friendly and she wants you to have her address she'll tell you.'

'But she doesn't know mine,' I said cunningly. 'She can't get in touch with me even if she wants to.'

There was no sympathy, no glimmer of help.

'That's tough,' the bloke said, 'but that's the way of it. We have to be pretty strict on things like that or we wouldn't get any girls to work for us.'

'Can't you even tell me if she is with your Agency?'

Even that was some sort of a state secret. I don't know what they expected me to do, but asking for any information was like sidling up to the director of an atomic research place and asking him how things were going and had there been any good discoveries lately? A stony silence, a blank stare, a shake of the head.

'Sorry, sir ...'

'We can't tell you that, sir ...'

After a day and a half of it I slipped into a phone box and called Maurice Longford. It was a faint hope but any chance was better than nothing.

'Have you heard from Marie?' I asked when I'd finally got past his secretary and was speaking to him in person.

'No, I haven't,' he said indignantly. 'I'm most upset and disappointed about the way she let me down and I hope you'll tell her so when you see her. I had to bring in another girl right at the last minute for that set of photographs she promised to do for me and she wasn't in the least bit as capable as Marie. What I wanted—'

'You've no idea where she might go?' I broke in, cutting short the stream of words.

'If I had, I'd have been after her long before this,' he said. 'She used to make me a lot of money, you know, and I can't really afford—'

'I'll give her your love when I see her,'

I said, and rang off, suddenly sick of the sound of his mincing, horrible voice.

In fact, I was getting sick of most things. The endless tramping round London, dealing with birds who looked down their noses at me and blokes who thought I was some sort of queer. The continual feeling that the cops were going to get me. The fact that my money was running out fast, and in another two weeks at the longest I was going to have to find a job and probably give up any hope of ever finding the girl.

When I did, she was going to wish she'd never set eyes on those diamonds.

I was wishing already that I'd never had anything to do with them.

It wouldn't have been so bad, I thought, if something would happen to break the deadlock which had sprung up. I couldn't even go to see Sandra Howell and try to frighten her into keeping away from the police, because she wasn't in the phone book and I didn't know where she lived.

I could do nothing, other than wait, and carry on with the useless quest that I'd set myself.

It was the day after I'd called Longford that I spotted a newspaper placard on Oxford Street.

All it said was: 'New Clue To Murder Of Charmwear Chief.'

IV

Until then I'd almost forgotten Bannister's connection with Charmwear. That brought it back with a jolt, and remembering the Photofit picture I felt very conspicuous as I bought the paper. I needn't have worried because no one took any notice of me, but as I turned away I felt a hand close on my arm. I swung round, my lips twisting, my muscles tensing as I prepared for a fight, and the little character who was holding me started back, alarm showing in his eyes.

'Forgot your change,' he muttered. 'If

you don't want it, I'm not bothered.'

I mumbled something, grabbed the coins and walked off, angry with myself. If I was going to start behaving like this at every turn I might as well find the nearest cop and tell him who I was, because sooner or later someone was going to guess the reason for my odd behaviour and then there'd be trouble.

I turned down a side street and wandered away from the crowds. As soon as I could I stopped, unfolded the paper and took a quick look at it. It was worse than I thought, right on the front page under a big headline. Settling myself against the wall I started to read the story, and the further I got with it the colder I became and the more my heart thumped and banged around my ribs.

'Detectives investigating the murder of Charmwear chief Charles Bannister now have the name of a man they wish to interview. He is Wayne Edwards, an advertising executive, who is believed to have visited Mr Bannister at his home shortly before the robbery and killing. A police spokesman wouldn't reveal the source of the new information but he did say: "We would like to talk to Edwards. We think he can help us with our enquiries." '

I knew the source of his information all right, but that didn't get me anywhere. It was too late now. There was a paragraph giving details of the murder, for those who'd forgotten them, and a few more details about me, including a quote from Christie. He'd really spread himself, calling me a good kid, and suggesting that I must have got into bad company. That was a private crack at Marie, just for me, of course, and the sort of thing that he'd think was funny.

Underneath all this, they'd repeated the Photofit picture, and captioned it with my name.

Crumpling the paper, I stuffed it into a bin and stood undecided what to do. All my things were at the hotel, and as I'd no money to buy any more I was going to have to go back there; the best thing was to go now and clear out before that stupid desk clerk saw the paper and remembered too much.

He looked at me strangely when I walked in. There was a tenseness about him and a set expression on his face that should have warned me, but didn't. All I did was stare right back at him then raise my eyebrows in enquiry. He looked away fast. When I was part way up the stairs I turned round suddenly and gave him a jeering grin when I caught him looking at me again.

Smiling was the last thing I felt like doing.

Maybe I had some queer idea in my mind that if only I could act as though things were still normal they'd really become normal.

As soon as I was in the corridor which led to my room I began to run along it, as noiselessly as I could. I could tell from the way he'd behaved that he'd recognized me and now that I was back in the hotel there was no telling how much time I'd have. He'd probably be onto the cops by now, and all I'd be able to do would be to throw my things into my suitcase and clear out.

This was how it was going to be for a long time, perhaps for the rest of my life. Safety for a few days and then on the run again. If only I had the money from the sale of those diamonds, I thought, I'd be able to get out of the country and hide for a year or two until everyone had forgotten me.

But I had no money, other than a few paltry pounds.

I thrust the key into the lock, turned it and saw the man sitting on the bed.

He was so obvious that he might as well have had the word 'cop' stencilled on his forehead.

Before he could move I slammed the

door shut again and turned the key, flinging it to the far end of the corridor. As I pounded down the stairs the desk clerk moved out with more speed than I would have given him credit for and stood right in my path. With him was the ex-Army type, a glint in his eyes as if he thought he was watching a charging native who was soon going to learn the power of the white man.

I didn't slow down. Jumping the last five stairs I arrived in the entrance hall moving like a cannonball, and the desk clerk tried to swing out of my way. He must have used up most of his energy coming round to the stairs, because he was nowhere near fast enough and I hit him with my shoulder, slamming him back against the desk so hard that the wood creaked in protest.

Or it could have been his bones.

From the corner of my eye I saw the other man coming forward in a crouching run, his hands low down as if he was holding a bayonet. I turned towards him and saw that he was grinning. The heavy book in which I'd signed the false name was on the desk. Grabbing it I flung it into his face and as he went over with a yell I saw the cop coming down the stairs.

He had a mate with him. Both of them were tough looking burly types, and I knew that once they got hold of me I wouldn't have any chance at all.

I jumped for the door. Someone was coming in, a stranger intending to book a room. He stood back as he saw the hurry I was in, then peered through the door into the entrance hall. The last I saw of him he was walking rapidly in the other direction, ignoring me.

I wished that the cops were doing the same thing. I was running as fast as I could, my feet beating on the pavement, merging with the sounds of the twin sets of cop feet hurrying after me. They seemed to be gaining and I knew that I'd no hopes of keeping up that speed for long. My car was on that croft a couple of hundred yards away, but even if I could have reached it they'd have been on me before I'd had time to get in and start the engine.

Bright flecks of light came in front of my eyes. I tried to dodge out of the way of them before I realized what was causing them, my mind was in such a state.

On the other side of the street I saw two blokes stop to stare at us. One of the cops yelled something, and as the younger of the pair started across the road I groaned aloud. If he joined in, fresh and enthusiastic, I might as well give up. They were certain to catch me, and that would be the end of it. Already my legs were failing, and I had to force them to take each step with a conscious effort. My chest ached, and I reckoned that if I reached the next street corner, still a good way from my car, I'd be lucky.

Behind me, an engine purred. I half expected a police car, but the thing that came alongside me was a pale pink

American job, so big that a travelling circus could have got inside it with seats to spare. With that chasing me as well I wondered why I was bothering to run, but I carried on, keeping my face turned away from it as if that would lessen the chances of the driver realizing it was me they were chasing.

'Get in here, pal,' he urged softly. 'You've no other way of getting out of trouble.'

He was right, but that didn't make me any keener to do it. Even the cops were better than taking a car ride with Singer.

Chapter Four

Mister Singer.

He grinned at me from inside that huge pink car as if he knew exactly what I was thinking. I turned to glare at him, too breathless to say anything, then looked away again. I didn't have much hope of getting away, but in the circumstances I'd rather take my chance with the cops than get into a car with him.

'You're a fool, Edwards,' he said, cruising alongside me, the engine revving as he slipped the clutch to keep down to my speed. 'You've no chance. Get in here and you're laughing.'

I swallowed.

Behind me, the sounds of the chase were very loud. The two cops who'd been hiding in my room were quite a distance behind, and if there'd only been those two I might have managed to escape; as it was, there was the newcomer to bear in mind, a lot fresher than any of us, tough and muscular, the type who'd think nothing of starting a brawl with me just so he could boast about it later to his mates in the pub, or his girlfriend.

In the state I'd be in when he got me, he'd be sure to win, and it was that thought which almost decided me to jump into Singer's car.

While that would get me away from here, it wouldn't solve another problem. Prison might be bad, but arguing with Singer could be fatal. I hesitated, wondering if he'd shout through the window again. The car was visible out of the corner of my eye, and as I tried to make up my mind I suddenly saw it draw a few yards ahead. My mouth opened to yell after him. The front end wallowed up and down like a hippo in a pool as he slammed on the brakes, then I had other things to think about.

A hand grabbed my collar.

A voice said: 'Got you!'

I pulled against the grip, but I was too weak and out of breath. He stuck his knee into my back, forcing me down onto the pavement. It was the young chap who'd joined in the chase, and he was behaving now as if he'd been waiting all day for a chance to get into a brawl. I struggled to get free, trying to get him down with me, but it didn't do any good; it was like wrapping my arms round a tree trunk and trying to knock it over. My teeth set in a savage grimace as I strained against him, he started to grin and not far away the cops were closing in on us, one of them yelling something. The words made a funny buzzing sound in my head.

From somewhere a fresh set of footsteps hammered in above the noise that everyone else was making. I was aware of a confused scrambling around me, a grunt, another yell from the cops. Before I could figure out what was happening I was grabbed by the collar and yanked to my feet.

'Come on, Edwards,' Singer said into my ear. 'You're not so far gone that you can't stand up.'

I shook my head dazedly. He sucked in his breath then hustled me across the pavement, thrust me in at the passenger door of his car, slammed it and skipped round to his own side. As he moved off the young tough who'd caught up with me jumped forward. Singer never even slowed down. He drove off as if there was no one in his path, the lad's hand slapped against the bonnet with a dull clanging sound, and there was a faint scream. I felt a slight bump on the side of the car, and saw him slipping to one side.

'Look, Singer—'

'Mister Singer,' he said absently, looking in his mirror, revving the car through the gears and making a getaway like he was leaving the grid at Le Mans. 'You look out of breath, pal.'

I was still gasping, to be sure. My brain

was whirling. I couldn't see any way out of the trap I was in but if I wanted to come through this alive I'd have to find one. Not only that, but everything I owned was still at the hotel and the cops would soon find out that it was my car on that croft. I had nothing at all now other than the clothes I was wearing and the few quid in my pocket, but if I didn't deal with Singer that wouldn't matter at all.

Money melts in the place where he wanted to send me.

I glanced at him out of the corner of my eye. He was as gaily dressed as ever. Red, purple and green striped trousers. A yellow shirt. A wide, flowered tie, but no mention of Rupert Bear anywhere. That surprised me, but I thought it better not to comment on it.

He was so intent on his driving that he didn't know I was watching him. He was setting a fair pace through the traffic, using the weight of the big car to bulldoze his way through places where I'd never have tried to get my own car. I started to sweat at the thought of what might happen if we hit anything, but then I relaxed. It didn't matter either way. I was caught, and whatever happened was beyond my control.

Gradually we came out of central London, and he slowed down a trifle.

'Good job that I was keeping an eye on you,' he said in a conversational tone. 'You'd never have got out of that on your own.'

'It might be good for you.' My voice was bitter. 'I don't imagine that it's so good for me.'

He grinned.

'You never know, pal.'

'What do you mean?'

'You sound as if you're still out of breath,' he said, grinning. 'If you trained like me you wouldn't have worried about a little chase like that.'

'What do you want?'

'Tell you what's the best thing to do,'

he said. 'You sit back there and get your breath in some sort of order. We'll talk when we get to my place. I remember when I worked on the building sites we once had a compressor that made a funny sort of whistling sound like you're making now. Coupla days later it packed up and never ran again.'

He laughed, smacked down into third gear as the traffic lights changed in front of him and then accelerated away. From the way the car surged for a moment I'd say that the back wheels spun. We shaved past a bus which was just starting off, cut between a couple of cars that were in front of Singer, getting in his way, and then settled down in top gear again.

'Got to judge it right,' he told me. 'It's no good unless you know the width of your car.'

'Suppose you quit the small talk,' I said savagely. 'There's only one reason why you pulled me out of there and that was so you could get the five thousand quid you think

I'm trying to chisel you out of.'

He glanced at me. He looked at me for so long that I thought he'd forgotten he was driving a car, but then he glanced back at the road.

'Could be,' he agreed. 'Like I said, we'll talk about it over a drink at my place.'

We came to another set of lights. There was no going through these on the amber because there was too much traffic on the road which ran across. Singer stopped, and as he did so I reached for the door handle.

'Thanks for the ride,' I said as I opened it. 'I'll get out here and walk the rest of the way.'

One of his massive hands grabbed me by the neck, his fingers wrapping themselves round it from behind, so big that they touched my throat and almost met. He pulled me back against him as if I were a bird whom he'd been trying to make for weeks. With his other hand he reached round me and slammed the door shut. The lights changed. I struggled, trying to get away from him, and the driver of a lorry behind gave a long blast on the horn.

'Don't try anything funny,' Singer warned me. 'If you do and I hit anything I'll make sure you get it bad. And don't forget that the cops'll come and you won't have a chance.'

'You don't want to see the cops any more than I do,' I muttered, but I stopped struggling just the same, and leaned back in my seat.

He moved off. It wasn't worth trying to get away. Even if I got through the door he'd still be in his car, and the memory of how he'd run down that tough was still fresh in my mind.

Neither of us spoke again during the journey. After about twenty minutes he turned into a road that was so narrow I don't think the car would have fitted down it, but it didn't slow him up much. A brick wall on each side shaved past with maybe six inches clearance, and here and there I caught a glimpse of a doorway. I prayed that no one would step out of any of the doorways, then about fifty yards further on the road widened out and Singer stopped alongside a new Rover whose paintwork glistened in the sunshine.

We got out.

'If you're thinking of running for it, don't,' he said, reaching into his pocket and poking a gun at me. 'I'll get you before you reach the end of the road.'

'You'll never have that five thousand quid if you shoot me.'

'Suppose you give up yapping and listen to what other people have to say,' he suggested. 'You never know, you could learn a lot that way.'

We walked along the road like buddies. The houses were old, crumbling mansions which were different from the one where I'd had my flat only in that they were a little smarter. Not much, but enough to be noticeable. Here and there one of them had been painted, generally a bright red or yellow which looked fine now but which would seem even scruffier than before when it had had chance to get dirty, and at one of them across the road someone had even weeded the garden and cut the lawn.

No one had painted the one where Singer lived, nor had they done its garden. He took me up a steep flight of dreary, dark stairs, along a dusty passage and into a flat. When he'd closed the door he waved towards a cabinet in one corner of the room.

'Drinks are over there. Pick what you like.'

'You sound like a pitcher on the market,' I said as I opened the door and grabbed a bottle and a couple of glasses.

'Back in the old days I used to stand the markets,' he said, 'so that isn't surprising.'

'Why didn't you stay there?' I sneered. 'Who knows, you might have been able to cope with that.'

'Looks as if I'm coping pretty well now,

doesn't it?' He laughed, took the glass from me and tipped the whisky down his throat. He might have been pouring it down a drain. When he'd got rid of one glassful he poured himself another one straight away from the bottle which I'd left handy on a small table.

The room was neat enough, but the jumble of furniture and the hideous wallpaper wouldn't have won any acclaim in the glossy housekeeping magazines. A colour television set stood near the window. Hanging over the back of a chair was the Rupert Bear tie he'd been wearing when I'd first met him, the one that said 'Mr Singer is Here' on it. I grinned at it, then looked away.

The breathless feeling had gone now, my chest wasn't aching any more and there were no coloured lights in front of my eyes. I drank the whisky slowly. In a few minutes I was going to feel something like normal, and that was the time to try and get out. Not before. Until then, he'd be certain to grab me, and I didn't want to feel those fingers on my neck again; next time, they might squeeze a mite too hard.

So, I had to let him talk until I felt ready to make a dash for it. If I played it right I'd get out, and not even the gun would stop me. Besides, he'd chucked that on the table as if it had been nothing but the evening paper, so it didn't appear that he was relying on it; although I couldn't reach it from where I was sitting, there was nothing to stop me looking at it.

Singer grinned at me.

'Don't get ideas, Edwards,' he said. 'I'm the only one who gets those.'

'You make it sound like the actress and the bishop,' I told him. 'What idea have you got right now?'

He tossed down the remains of his second glass of whisky and got up to pour himself another.

'My idea is that there's been a little bit of monkey business along the line, and we're going to talk about it. I suppose you thought it was smart to leave that flat of yours and go to that dump of a hotel?'

'It was either that or having visitors that I didn't want.'

'Meaning me or the cops?' Singer sat down again and hunched forward in his chair, staring at me and keeping the glass of whisky in his hand.

'Both of you,' I replied. 'To me one was as bad as the other.' My eyes wandered to the door while I was talking; the distance from my chair to it looked greater every minute.

Singer tipped some more whisky down his throat, banged the glass down next to the bottle and then leaned back. He settled himself comfortably, then said:

'Let's talk about my five thousand quid for starters, shall we? I can see you haven't forgotten it by the way you keep mentioning it.'

'Now listen, Singer,' I said. 'It's no use talking to me about that because—'

'Because you haven't got it,' he finished.

'I know pal, I know. That bird took you for a mug, didn't she? She can pick 'em like the kids pick daisies in the field, whole bunches of them, and then throw them away when she's finished with them. Mugs, you and me both.'

I swallowed, looking at him without really understanding what he'd said. He didn't seem to be joking, but with someone like him you could never tell, and it was dangerous to take anything he said as the truth.

'How much do you know about it?' I asked eventually; it seemed to be the safest thing to say.

'As much as you, or maybe a little more. I knew what night you were pulling that job and as soon as I read about the murder in the papers I went round to see Marie. She wasn't in. I gave it a few hours then called again, thinking that maybe she was out somewhere. When there was still no answer I got into her flat, took a look round and soon realized that she didn't intend coming back. I reckoned that the pair of you had done a flit together.'

I gave him a faint smile.

'From the way you were talking a few minutes ago I gather that you've changed your mind.'

'That's right,' he said, nodding. 'A couple of things didn't fit in when I got to thinking about it. I know Marie, and I know what she's like. I should have got payment in advance from her, but I knew she hadn't got it and if you never take a chance you never get anywhere, do you? I took her on trust, and that was where I slipped up, but I guessed that if anyone was going to skip away it would be her, and I couldn't see why she'd bother to lumber herself with you.'

'Thanks very much.'

'You'd have cramped her style, pal. The other thing that struck me as funny was that there was no mention of her in any of the papers. I read them all, and everyone said the same thing, that a bloke had broken in and killed Bannister when he nearly caught him. Marie could have been a ghost for all they cared about her, and I worked out that if no one had seen her there'd have been no need for her to run.'

'She could have got scared.'

He shrugged.

'It's possible, but it doesn't square with what she's done in the past. Besides, she was keen on that modelling jazz, even if it didn't make her much money, but she wasn't so stuck on you that she'd have thrown it all up for you.'

'That's what you think,' I said. 'If I'd been on the run with thirty thousand pounds worth of stones she'd have come after me.'

He grinned. His teeth were large and white, with occasional specks of black on them. They looked like a row of dice in his mouth.

'If you'd gone on the run, pal, she'd never have let you take those stones with you. Either you'd have run on your own, without them, or you'd both have stayed, but one thing's sure. She wouldn't have gone on the run with you.'

He was right. From what I knew of her, which didn't seem so much now, I could say that running over London with the cops not far behind, like I'd been doing, wasn't in her line. I don't know if I could have reasoned it out like Singer, but it was there just the same.

'So when I found out that she'd gone I guessed after a while that she'd pulled out on you too. I came round to see you and find out if that was right, but you weren't there.'

Too right I wasn't, but I didn't intend upsetting him any more by telling him that while he'd been beating down my door I'd been climbing out of a window on the other side of the house. A sudden thought struck me.

'How did you know my address?' I asked suspiciously.

'Don't get worried. Finding things out is my job, remember. That's why you owe me the five thousand quid, because I found out all those details about Bannister for you. A little thing like that is nothing to me.'

'I'd still like to know how you did it,' I insisted.

'I asked Marie, days ago, before you ever did the job,' he said wearily. 'Does it matter now?'

'It could have done,' I said. 'What are your plans now that you know Marie's got the diamonds and walked out on me?'

'I aim to talk about it for a while, like we're doing now. Who shopped you to the cops?'

'Who do you think?'

'I don't think anything,' he said sharply. 'That's why I asked.'

'That bird who was at Bannister's at the time, the one you forgot to tell me about. She—'

'I didn't forget to tell you about

anything,' he broke in. 'As far as I knew Bannister was on his own. He must have fixed her up at the last minute. Tough for you but there's nothing I can do about it. Did she see you?'

'She saw me,' I said. 'There was something about it in the papers at the time, and she gave them that description. She also saw me about two weeks earlier, when I went round on some business of Christie's. That's how she knew my name, and she must have remembered it and passed it on to the cops.'

Sandra Howell and the way she'd tried to blackmail me was something else that I was keeping quiet about. I figured that by going to the cops as she'd threatened she'd done all the damage that she could and I wouldn't be hearing from her again. In any case, Singer thought that he knew everything, and I had an idea that it might be useful to keep something back, even if I couldn't see what good it was going to be to me.

'The point is,' Singer said, throwing one leg over the arm of his chair and settling back, 'what are you going to do? You killed a bloke to get those diamonds. The cops are on your back, you've lost the stuff, you've lost Marie and I'm chasing you for five thousand quid. Any bright ideas in your head about how to handle it?'

'Throwing myself off the Tower Bridge might be a start,' I said, with a feeble attempt at a joke.

'That wouldn't solve anything. You'll have to get out and do something about it.'

'There isn't much I can do,' I said savagely, still angered by the fact that I was in a trap. 'If there was do you think I'd be sitting here yapping to you?'

'Maybe not.'

'And how did you know I was at that hotel?'

'Easy.' He grinned again. 'When I first found that Marie had gone I had the same idea as you. I went round the model agencies. I happened to see you going into one and I kept tabs on you. It was just luck, I guess.'

'I bet you didn't get a lead to Marie at any of those places, did you?'

'Toffee nosed bitches at most of them,' he said. 'Wouldn't even tell you the time unless you paid them commission.'

I nodded, and he pursed his lips, staring at me intently.

'If you really want to find her,' he said, 'I think I know how you can do it.'

I didn't answer him.

'One thing that I always do when I start working with people is find out all about them,' he went on. 'I knew about you and Alf Christie, for instance, how you argued with him about Marie. I knew that you hated that punk Maurice Longford. I knew that Marie had made you buy a car, that she was screwing you for every penny you had and that you couldn't really afford her. That's why you took the diamonds, isn't it?'

'Get on with it,' I said, my nerves on edge. 'While we're sitting here talking the cops are looking for me. And you knocked that bloke down, too. What happens if they've got your number?'

'There's mud all over the plates,' he said easily. 'Remind me to go and wash it off sometime.'

'So you think they won't come here?' I sneered. 'That's what I thought when I went to that crummy hotel, and look where it got me.'

'It'll get you to Marie, pal, if you play it the right way. One thing I know about that bird that very few other people know is the answer to all our problems. Longford doesn't know, Christie doesn't know and you don't know. But I found it out and it's going to lead me to thirty thousand quid.'

I thought he was spinning a line, but I wanted to hear it just the same.

'Tell me,' I suggested.

'She has a cottage in Cornwall,' he said.

'It's my bet that she's gone down there because she thinks she'll be safe, but I could find her in a few hours.'

My throat felt tight.

Singer gave me a jeering smile.

'Well?' he said. 'Are you interested in working with me or not?'

II

Something about his voice told me that he was speaking the truth. Anyway, as far as I could see there was no point to his lying to me about something like that; what possible reason could he have for wanting to get me down to a cottage in Cornwall other than that Marie was actually there? If he wanted to kill me there were plenty of places that were just as lonely and which were nearer at hand; if he was trying to send me off on a wild-goose chase, it didn't make sense.

What I was more wary of was this offer to work with him. I could foresee

160

complications if I took him up on that, but I decided that for the time being it would be easier to let him think that he was playing me along.

'If everyone else is so ignorant, how do you know about it?' I asked.

'I've told you, I make it my business to find out things like that. I've got a lot of friends, I ask questions and I remember the things I find out. You've got to agree that I didn't have any trouble getting you all that stuff about Bannister, did I?'

'I don't know,' I said off-handedly, 'all you did as far as I'm concerned was come to me with the results. How the hell do I know how much trouble you had to go to? If it was as little as you're trying to tell me now I think that you're getting your five grand for nothing.'

'I haven't got it yet,' he said softly. 'And when I do, it's going to be more than five grand. If I tell you where Marie's cottage is, I want a half share.'

'Half!' I jerked forward in my chair.

'Listen, Singer, I don't know—'

'Mister Singer,' he said. 'Don't ever forget that. Why shouldn't I get half? Don't forget that without me there wouldn't be anything to share.'

'Maybe not, but—'

'Half or nothing. Take it or leave it.'

'Look, Mr Singer,' I said, 'before we start arguing let's get the basics over, shall we?'

'Such as?'

'Why are you telling me this? If you're so sure that you know where the diamonds are why don't you go down and get them?'

He stared at me, his leg still over the arm of the chair, his foot swinging casually in the air.

'That's a good question,' he said, 'and there's a good answer to it.'

'Let's hear it.'

He gave an amused smile.

'You're not taking any chances, are you?' he said. 'The point is that if the cops got you, one of the things you'd blab to them is all about me. I know that I stand out in a crowd, but I can't help that, it's the way I am. Because of it, though, I wouldn't last half an hour if they ever put out a description of me.'

His voice dropped slightly.

'The other thing is that if I went down there and got those stones something might happen to Marie while I was doing it. Get what I mean?'

I got what he meant, all right. A little touch of the Bannisters, with Marie on the receiving end.

'If that happened,' he went on, 'you might be tempted to do a deal with the cops, save your neck at the expense of mine, that sort of thing.'

'So you want me tied up in it to make sure that doesn't happen?'

He shrugged.

'Let's say that I'm honest and I want you to have your share, pal. You've worked for it as much as I have. More, probably.'

I didn't go for that bull, but I wanted to string him along. If I didn't, I'd no illusions about what would happen to me before I got anywhere near Marie or any diamonds again. And if Singer thought he was getting any half share off me he wasn't as wise in the ways of the world as he was trying to make out. As soon as I got my hands on those stones I intended to keep the lot. Handing over half of them to a joker like Singer didn't figure in my plans at all.

Nor did I care what happened to Marie. Not now. To me, she was just another bird, and if she got in the way of something that I happened to be doing, it was too bad for her. Skipping out like she had had finished any feeling that I might have had for her, though she was so vain that when we met again she wouldn't realize that and would start to pull all her old tricks.

Let her try. If I didn't take care of her, Singer would.

With things as they were, arguing about

the percentage that Singer was going to get was academic as far as I was concerned, but if I didn't put up some sort of a show it would look suspicious. I argued with him for a few minutes more then gave in, accepting defeat with an ill grace, just the sort of attitude I guessed he'd expect me to take.

'That's the way of it, pal,' he said. 'One thing goes wrong, then another, but half of the money's better than the whole of nothing, which is what you had before I picked you up. If I don't give you the address of Marie's cottage, that's all you'll still have.'

'You'll be coming down there with me?' I asked.

'I'm not that stupid,' he said. 'I'll be right at your side.'

'When were you thinking we should set off?'

He grinned.

'I thought you'd see it my way. It's a little late to start off now but what I suggest is that we drive down tomorrow and reach the cottage in nice time to spend the night there. We'll come back the day after, thirty thousand quid richer. Fifteen thousand each.'

'Just making sure I get the point,' I said bitterly. 'I hope you can get that much for them.'

'If they're as good as you said they were I'll manage all right. I could even sell them for more, I don't know.'

'Fifteen thousand will do me,' I said. 'Where is this cottage?'

'A little place you won't have heard of called Tregarth. It's on the coast, in the old tin country, and the cottage is about quarter of a mile from the village, looking out over the sea.'

'Sounds nice,' I said. 'How did Marie come to get hold of a cottage like that?'

'Search me. I think she must have had a boyfriend who knew someone in that line. I thought you'd have learned by now that a girl like Marie can get most things if she puts her mind to it.'

He unhooked his leg from over the chair and crossed to a tall cupboard at the back of the room. From it he took a map which he spread out on the table. Tucked inside the map was a sheet of paper with a rough sketch plan of the Tregarth area drawn on it with a felt-tipped pen. From it, it was possible to work out exactly where the cottage was and after a few minutes study I reckoned that I'd probably be able to find it without Singer's help; that would probably be a vital part of whatever plan I dreamed up.

'So there you are,' he said, folding up the map and tossing it onto a chair. 'We leave tomorrow. You can stay here for the night if you want.'

'Assuming that I'll be safe.'

'You'll be a bloody sight safer here than you will be roaming about London with every cop on the streets looking out for you.' He gave me a jeering smile. 'Quit panicking. If it'll make you feel any happier you can wedge a chair under the door handle.'

I did just that. We didn't spend the most cheerful of evenings, looking at the map, listening to the news on the local radio to see if there was any mention of me (which there wasn't), and making desultory conversation. I was glad when it drew later and I could reasonably say that I was going to bed.

The chair pushed under the handle made me feel safer, but not much.

I knew that there was some trickery about Singer's offer. He wasn't so big-hearted as to be anxious that I got my share of the money, nor was he cutting me in on the diamonds simply because he was afraid that I'd do a deal with the cops if he didn't, but although I turned it over and over in my mind I couldn't see what he was up to. Not that I was too bothered what it was. What really interested me was my own plan to get hold of all the diamonds for myself; I worked on it until I fell asleep, but I didn't get very far.

The noise of Singer clumping about the flat woke me up. I listened to him for a while, thinking that he sounded far too lively for that time in the morning, then I dressed quickly, shaved and went into the living room.

He looked up when I came in, then flung the morning paper at me.

'You're famous, pal,' he said. 'Have a look on the front page.'

I knew what I was going to see long before I'd turned the pages back to the beginning. My own face, the inevitable Photofit, altered now that a couple of cops had actually seen me. There was no doubt as to who it was, and no doubt either that any cop who saw me would recognize me at once. My heart turned inside out. With things like that floating about I wasn't going to get very far, either in London or Cornwall.

'You don't get much of a mention,' I said to Singer. 'Seems like no one saw very much of you.'

'All too interested in you,' he said. 'That's a pity, really. You've already had your picture in the paper once and I figured I was due for a turn.' He glared at me with assumed anger then burst into a loud guffaw of laughter.

'There's that character you knocked down,' I said, glancing at the rest of the page and seeing a photograph of the young tough who'd joined in the chase. 'You put him in hospital, but they're expecting to discharge him today.'

Singer nodded.

'He'll live. There's still something you haven't seen.'

There was, too. A side headline, immediately below my photograph.

'Five Thousand Pound Reward Offered.'

'Charmwear have laid that on,' Singer said. 'Five grand to anyone who turns you in. If the diamonds weren't worth a lot more than that I might have taken a chance myself.'

He laughed again but I was too busy reading the story to take any notice of him. This meant that everyone, not only the cops but all kinds of people who fancied their luck at making what they thought would be a bit of easy money would be looking for me.

At the end of the item it said:

'Police chiefs slammed the idea of the reward. A spokesman commented: "We do not urge the public to have a go. This man has killed once and is likely to kill again if he is cornered." '

'It must be a great feeling to know that you're worth so much,' Singer commented.

'Yeah,' I said, tossing the paper into the empty grate. 'It makes me feel like a cross between a wild animal and Billy The Kid.'

III

It was raining when we left for Cornwall, not hard but a light drizzle which was so fine it was almost like a mist. The windscreen wipers on Singer's big pink car slapped from side to side, and from time to time I gave the windows a quick wipe with a bright yellow duster which I found on a ledge below the dashboard. The idea of the reward still worried me, but all Singer did when I talked about it was laugh.

'The public are thick,' he said. 'They've no more chance of recognizing you than I have of being Prime Minister. I should forget it. If you ask me, it's just some publicity gimmick that Charmwear have dreamed up.'

'According to the paper it's to show their respect to Bannister.'

He waved his arm airily.

'It's a stunt,' he insisted. 'You should know all about things like that if you worked in advertising.'

'They could get a lot of publicity for five thousand quid.'

'Maybe they could, but in the end they'd

get a bill which they'd have to pay. This way they get coverage in every national paper without paying a cent. They don't really expect anyone to claim that reward so I should quit worrying.' He glanced out of the window and then back at me. 'From the way you're driving this thing I'd say that you want to think more about that than what the cops are doing.'

We were using his car because, of course, mine was in the hands of the police after I'd to abandon it yesterday at that hotel. According to a bulletin on the radio they were going over it carefully, but I knew that I hadn't left anything in it that would help them or tell them anything that they didn't already know, so I wasn't worrying about that. Singer was letting me drive. I suppose he felt safer that way than he would if he'd had me sitting next to him for three hundred miles with nothing to do but look out of the window and dream up plans to get rid of him.

'There's another thing,' I said. 'What do

I do if the cops stop me for speeding for something?'

'You'll have to make sure they don't stop you. Just drive like you were taking the test again and I was the examiner. That way no one's going to get into trouble.'

'And we aren't going to get to Cornwall so fast either.'

'We're not in any hurry. I'd rather get there than have some copper come nosing around halfway, just because he thinks you were going too fast or you didn't stop at a zebra crossing. Take it easy and don't worry.'

I'd given a lot of thought as to how I could double cross him, but I hadn't had any brilliant ideas. All I could do now was wait and see if anything turned up; there was a long way to go yet, and even if nothing turned up on the journey there was no telling what might happen when we got to this cottage of Marie's.

Driving his big car was a lot different to driving the old heap that I'd had. It needed a lot more space on the road for one thing, but the respect which drivers of smaller stuff showed to me made up for that; the thing that took some getting used to after the heavy, suet pudding acceleration of my own car was that if I gave this too much gas in low gear the back wheels would spin. The first time I did that was an accident; the second was deliberate, but when I saw Singer give me a sharp glance, and spotted the outline of a gun in his pocket, I decided to cool it a little.

There was more traffic than either of us had expected, and the rain, which steadily increased the further West we got, didn't help to keep the traffic flowing smoothly. We stopped for lunch and tea, and as it began to grow dark we decided to pull up for some coffee.

'Should be there in a couple of hours now,' Singer said, glancing at his watch as I drove into the park of a small transport cafe, somewhere out in the wilds.

175

I nodded. I was stiff from the hours of driving that I'd already put in, but I knew there was no chance of getting him to take the wheel. If he had, I reckon he'd have wrecked us up before we'd gone more than a mile; the nearer we got to Cornwall, the more tense he became.

As we went into the cafe we met a bunch of truckers coming out. I brushed against Singer as I moved to avoid them, keeping my face turned into the shadows, and I could feel him trembling with excitement.

It wasn't a big place, just a large wooden hut with plastic topped tables scattered about, a beat up old juke box with a sign on it, out of order, a glittering chromium coffee machine, all the usual sort of stuff. The rain drummed on the roof, and I shook myself like a cat to dry myself.

'Bad night,' the counter hand said as he gave me the coffees.

I grunted something. There was no hint of panic or recognition on his face, but we still sat down at a table well to one side, where we were out of the way and where there was a handy door to get out of.

We were halfway through a couple of bacon sandwiches when two cops walked in.

No one took any notice of them except me. Sweat broke out on my forehead. Singer had his back to them but my expression must have given away that something was wrong, and under cover of wiping his mouth he looked round.

'For God's sake stop looking as if you've seen the old family ghost,' he muttered to me when he'd turned back. 'Try and behave normally. They can't know you're in here, so they're not looking for you. Probably they want a smoke for an hour.'

'I'm not so sure.' I slopped some coffee into my saucer in my haste, and turned my face away.

Neither of the cops made any attempt to go to the counter. The counter hand wiped the top of it and looked at them. Rain dripped off their hats and made puddles on the floor, then one of the cops glanced towards me, slapping his leather driving glove against his leg.

I pretended I'd dropped something on the floor and stooped to pick it up. Singer was still eating placidly, as if nothing was wrong, and then the cops moved, making their way slowly to the counter.

'Doing much tonight, Stan?' one of them asked.

'Not so bad considering the weather. No one wants to stop when it's raining.'

'We'll have to get out of here,' I muttered to Singer.

'Not right now,' he said, looking worried. 'It'll be too suspicious.'

'I don't give a damn what's suspicious,' I snarled. 'It'll look more suspicious if they see me sitting here.'

One of the cops said: 'All truckers, are they? Get much private car trade?'

'A bit.' I saw him glance towards us, and thought that he was going to point us out. He didn't.

'I see there's a car outside in the park,' the other cop said, just a shade too casually. I knew then that they were looking for me, and they'd come in because they'd recognized Singer's car as the same type as the one that had picked me up yesterday.

The counter hand was saying something, but I didn't wait to hear what it was. Near where we were sitting was the emergency exit I'd seen earlier, and if this wasn't an emergency, nothing was.

'Come on,' I said to Singer and stood up.

The cops saw me then.

One of them started forward, Singer jumped up, and as he did so I shoved the table into him. He folded over in the middle and I grabbed my chair, broke it over his head and then flung the bits at the cops.

Singer was sprawled on the floor, his face twisted with pain and rage. I jumped for the door, scrabbled at the handle which held it closed and which seemed to have been designed so that it wouldn't open quickly, freed it after what felt like an hour and ran out into the chill night air.

The rain teemed down. It drummed on the ground, and made an odd, tinny noise on the lids of a row of nearby dustbins.

I was at the side of the hut. To reach Singer's car I had to pass the front door, and I expected the cops to run out. Neither of them did. From inside the cafe I could hear the sound of shouting, though Singer's voice wasn't there. As I reached the car and yanked the keys from my pocket the thin string on which they were threaded broke and they fell into the mud at my feet. I grovelled for them, and saw from the corner of my eye that one of the cops had appeared, a gash on his face where a piece of the chair had caught him.

My fingers closed on something hard in the mud. It felt like one of the keys, but as I uncovered it I saw that it was a stone. I flung it at the cop, and he swerved to one side, but kept coming.

I scrabbled frantically. He was very close by the time I found them, and there was just time to thrust the key into the lock and get the door open before I felt the cop's hand on my shoulder.

Knowing that if I delayed long enough for his mate or Singer to come out nothing could save me I rammed my elbow back into his ribs. He gave a funny, strangled grunt, but didn't let go of me. Desperately I hit him again, and felt his fingers slip on my wet sweater. I kicked backwards, his hold vanished and I fell across the driving seat.

The ignition light glowed as I turned the key. I used the steering wheel to pull myself upright. As I gunned the motor and moved off, the door still swinging open, he grabbed the edge of it and I heard a crack as he almost broke the hinges.

I leaned over. His weight was too much for me to pull it closed, and I could see his blood smeared face twisted with satisfaction. He thought he had me, and when I saw his sidekick running across the park I knew that he wasn't far wrong.

I slammed the car into reverse. The sudden change of direction broke his hold, cinders flew up as I got bottom gear again and pulled round in the kind of turn a car that size was never intended to make. The other cop jumped back to avoid being cracked by the swinging door, and then I was racing over the bumpy ground towards the road.

Parked just inside the gate was the cop car.

If I could get a start on them they'd never catch me, not with all the horses under Singer's bonnet.

I was so busy thinking about how I was going to get away that I never switched on the wipers. The screen was streaked with water, and because of that I nearly didn't see the truck that was coming in until it was too late. The bright flash of its headlights jerked my thoughts back to what I was doing, together with the hiss of air brakes as it stopped, leaving a gap which was either big enough for me to get through or slightly too small.

I clenched my hands on the wheel. My face was damp with sweat. Most of the car shaved through the opening, but I'd forgotten about that door. It slammed against the front of the lorry and folded right back along the side of the car, then I was through. Not bothering about it I switched the wipers on and accelerated along the main road, the cold air whipping into the car and bringing the rain with it.

I was already soaked too much for that to matter, and the cold and wet helped to keep me alert after I'd been driving for so long. Rather than keep to the main road, where I'd easily be found, I turned off along a narrow lane, twisting about, the headlamps full on, and then after twenty minutes or so I stopped. It was still raining, but I couldn't see the lights of any other cars, and I reckoned that for the time being at least, I was safe.

If I was going to stay that way I'd either have to get another car, or get this door right.

I got out and the rain plastered my disordered hair to my head. The door was jammed firmly, and it was only by bracing one leg against the side of the car and giving a really good heave that I could free it. It moved stiffly. The impact with the truck had bent it out of shape, but I managed to get it closed eventually. There was no telling how long it would stay like that, because any sort of uneven road surface would cause it to fly open, and apart from being dangerous it also made the car too distinctive; any car that happened to be American and pink would be stopped, but it would be the one with the wrecked driver's door that would get the individual treatment.

Leaving that door closed I got in at the other side, slid across the seats and drove on slowly. Round one of the bends in the lane I came upon a car which had been run into a layby made where a farm gate opened onto the road. I was about to stop when I saw that the front end was smashed in; even if I could have made it run it would have stood out more than Singer's. I gave up, and drove on into Exeter.

I was luckier there. It wasn't all that late, and as the cinema crowds hadn't come out yet there was street after street of parked cars. I tried a few, found the inevitable one with a window left open and soon had the door unlocked and the engine running. Singer's heap ran easily into an entry where it would be out of the public eye, and I drove away in my new transport.

A few minutes later I passed a police patrol car. The driver ignored me. I grinned when I'd passed him, drove as quickly as I dared until I'd covered about fifty miles, then pulled up. I'd been driving almost continuously since leaving London, and although there was a need for haste I was

185

getting so tired that my eyes were closing as I went along. If I wasn't going to hit something well before I got anywhere near Tregarth I'd have to have a rest.

I ran the car into a layby and settled down for a sleep.

In a way, meeting those cops had been a stroke of luck from my point of view. It had enabled me to get away from Singer and leave him stranded, but there was still a danger that he'd tell them where I was going and they'd be waiting for me when I got there. From the other way of looking at it, though, there might be no reason why he should do that. He was a resourceful character, and from the way I'd dealt with him he wouldn't have much trouble spinning them a yarn that I'd been hitch hiking and he'd picked me up.

After all, they couldn't prove that the car they'd seen was the one that had picked me up. And if he kept his wits about him, he could make the story seem even more plausible by turning it round and saying that he was the hitch hiker and I'd stopped for him. That would let him out completely, and the more I thought about it the more certain I became that was what he'd do. As soon as he'd finished making statements to the cops and found himself another car he'd be after me, but I reckoned I'd have a clear couple of hours before he could start.

I slept for a while and felt better for it. The rain was still coming down, and the wind was gusting off the moors and across the exposed roads, making the little car scutter about, but by keeping the gas pedal right down and scarcely slowing for anything I covered the rest of the journey much more quickly than I'd hoped.

Tregarth was a typical Cornish place, looking forlorn and desolate in the rainy darkness. I didn't linger in the village but went straight through, following a lane which climbed out towards the coast, to where the cottage stood out gauntly against the sky. Before I reached it I pulled onto the grass verge and killed the engine, so that Marie wouldn't have any warning that anyone was about.

There were no lights in the cottage. I tramped across the wet grass, ignoring the rain and the wind which was sweeping in from the sea and howling round the cottage. On my right, was the sound of waves crashing against the foot of the cliff, and far out to sea a light was creeping through the darkness. I shuddered, glad that it wasn't me in a boat on a night like this.

Presently I came to a low stone wall which ran round the cottage and its garden. By the gate was a Cornish piskie, made of stone and about eighteen inches high; a signboard was in its hands, with the name Tregarth Cottage painted on it.

I went in through the gate, holding the latch so that it wouldn't click; a little sound like that would probably stand out, even above the racket of the storm. Facing me were two windows, but when I tried to see in through them I couldn't make out a thing, it was so dark inside. Round the side were more windows, but they were curtained, as I found when I rubbed the rain smeared glass to clear it.

It looked as if I wasn't going to get in.

Unless I knocked at the door, but that would be a stupid thing to do.

I licked the rain off my lips, and stood under the crude shelter of the eaves. The fact that no cops were anywhere about was proof enough for me that Singer had managed to put his story over, and a good indication that I could expect him to follow me here sooner or later. For all I knew, he could have been around then. The wind covered a lot of things, and near to where I was standing a broken drainpipe was gushing water, splashing it all over the path and onto the bedraggled flowers.

At the back was a rockery. I levered a smallish stone out of the soft, yielding soil, waited until a particularly big wave crashed against the cliff and gave one of the windows a smart tap. The glass broke cleanly, the big, jagged pieces were easily lifted out and it wasn't too much trouble to climb in.

Once out of the rain, I felt better, though it wasn't many moments before the eerie atmosphere of the place began to get through to me. The wind howled. The sea battered the cliffs. The rain clattered against the windows and gusted in through the pane I'd broken, sending the curtain billowing. At first I couldn't make out anything in the gloom, but my eyes gradually accustomed themselves to it and I gathered from the cooker in one corner that I was in the kitchen.

Moving softly and quietly I began to see if anyone was at home. There was no fresh food about, nothing at all in any of the cupboards, no sign that anyone had ever been here, apart from half a loaf of bread which I found and which was about as hard as the rock I'd used to smash the window.

Had Singer's plan in getting me here been deeper than I'd suspected? Could be, yet there was the rest of the cottage to explore still. Because there was no food in the kitchen it didn't mean that the cottage was empty, and even if it was, it didn't follow that the diamonds hadn't been left in some hiding place.

At the back of the room was a door. I opened it and stepped into what I imagined would be the living room.

As I did so the person hiding behind the door smashed a blow at my head.

IV

The attack was so sudden and unexpected that I had no chance to avoid it. I fell under the force of the blow. The cottage seemed to be a dark ball which was spinning round with me at the centre. As the spinning sensation increased the roar of the wind and sea swelled to an incredible noise, most of which was

191

probably the sound of my own blood pounding in my ears. Feebly I wagged my hand around, trying to get hold of something to use to pull myself up, and felt something with my fingertips.

A leg covered with nylon.

So I was fighting a girl.

Marie.

I was feeling better now, and as the sickness receded and the roaring sensation died away I heard another blow swishing towards me, a really vicious one, and if it had landed on my head, where it was meant to, I might not be here telling you this. Fortunately I had time to roll away and it hit my shoulder; I cried out as the pain streaked down my arm.

When I rolled over I could make out a dim girl-shape in front of me, looking enormous because of the angle at which I was seeing it. I grabbed for her, then had to roll away again as she swung a kick.

I caught her foot. She gave a little scream. I grinned in the darkness and twisted it as savagely as she'd been hitting me, not because I wanted to hurt her but because she was going to kill me if I didn't stop her soon. The rain had made my hands wet and slippery and there was water dripping into my eyes from my soaked hair, but it was a good powerful grip and she went over.

The crash as she thudded to the floor blotted out the noise of the storm outside.

She screamed.

'Do the lights work in this place?' I demanded, staggering to my feet and not really expecting an answer.

I didn't get one.

I knelt down again and groped at the dim figure, touching its feet cautiously and twisting one of them to see whether it was conscious or not, alive or dead. It didn't move but it was evident that she was only unconscious and might come round any minute.

Standing up again I went over to the wall and slapped my hand around in the most likely place to find the light switch, by the door. I discovered two, snapped them down and got a surprise which was even greater than the one I'd had when those cops had walked into the cafe.

I hadn't been fighting with Marie.

The girl at my feet was Sandra Howell.

Chapter Five

Now that I could see the room properly I discovered that it was smaller than I'd thought, and square, with a ragged carpet, a few old sticks of furniture and a vase of wilting flowers on the window sill, half hidden by the curtains. All the windows were closed, yet when the wind gusted the curtains moved slightly, as if there was a crack between the wall and the frame. It wasn't a cottage that was in good repair, whatever Marie used it for.

Sandra Howell was lying at my feet, and as I looked down at her she gave a faint groan, moving slightly. She was wearing a dark green blouse and jeans; when I knelt down and shook her, trying to bring her round, I noticed that they weren't so wet, so she must have been here some time.

Not only that, but there'd been no other car outside when I'd arrived. That meant she'd either walked here or been brought by someone else, who wasn't here now but might return any time.

Marie?

But as she had no car of her own that implied the existence of a third person. That didn't fit together, and in any case I couldn't see what link there could be between this girl and Marie.

She groaned again when I moved her, but her eyes remained closed. I gave her a really good shaking, like a dog worrying a rat, then went back into the kitchen. Whatever queer game was going on, Singer or the cops or someone unknown or all of them were likely to arrive at any time; if I was to get the full story out of her before that happened, there wasn't a minute to lose.

There was no bowl in the kitchen, but I did find a big sponge at the back of one of the cupboards. Dirt was caked on it and it was so hard it could have been made of cement. I ran cold water onto it. At first it was like wetting a duck, but gradually it began to soak in and I soon had it soft and pliable and full of water.

Sandra squirmed away when I squeezed it over her.

I twisted it, getting the last drops of water out of it, and eventually her eyes flickered open. There was a blank, dazed look in them, but that gradually cleared as I sneered down at her, until I could see that she knew what was going on, and didn't think much of it.

She shook her head. Whether she was trying to clear it or to get the water off her face I didn't know, nor care.

'Come on, you little nark,' I said to her, letting my voice come out from between my clenched teeth. 'It's time you and I had another talk.'

Her eyes glazed again, then cleared all at once. She knew who I was, and the clearness was replaced by fear when she realized she couldn't get away.

'What do you want here?' she muttered, her voice so hoarse that I could hardly make out the words.

'Just a talk with you, Sandra dear,' I said jeeringly. 'This time we should get on fine, and when we've finished you'll be able to tell your pals at Scotland Yard all about it. That's unless you get the same as Bannister.'

I got a real snap into my voice on that last sentence, and it jerked the last trace of the stupor away from her.

'What do you mean?' she demanded, though there was no doubt that she knew well enough.

'Let's skip that,' I said roughly, 'because there isn't a lot of time. What are you doing here?'

She started to get to her feet. I pushed her down again and grinned.

'Stay on the floor, baby. I can handle you better while you're there.'

'You think you're clever, don't you?'

'I know I'm clever, but that's got nothing to do with it. If I were you I'd answer the questions before I got hurt. You aren't in any position to give me a lot of lip, and don't forget it.'

I was starting to feel cold now that I'd been still for so long. The rain had soaked right through my clothes, my hair was stiff and wiry with the dried water and everytime I moved my shoes squelched. For the first time it occurred to me what a terrifying appearance I must have presented, and I grinned faintly at the thought.

Outside, I could still hear the rain coming down. It was showing no signs of letting up, and I began to get the feeling that instead of standing here talking we'd do better to find some spare wood and let me get on with making an ark while Sandra rounded up a few pairs of animals. The wind was howling too, and every so often there came the crash of a bigger than usual wave beating against the cliffs. Listening to it made me realize that when people say that the coast of Cornwall is slowly being worn away, they aren't joking. It beat me how anything could have stood up to a battering like that for a few minutes, let alone the thousands of years that those cliffs had been there.

Sandra was staring up at me, water from the sponge running down her face and dripping off her chin.

'Who brought you here?' I asked.

'No one. I walked.'

'You aren't wet.'

'I wasn't until you came,' she said, with a flash of spirit. 'Maybe that's because when I got here it wasn't raining.'

'When was that?'

'This afternoon. The rain didn't start until around teatime.'

I looked at her thoughtfully. There we were, with thirty thousand pounds worth of diamonds at stake and in imminent danger from the cops or Singer, and all we did was talk about the rain. Typically English.

'Who told you to come here?' Sandra demanded. 'I know you're after the diamonds, but what made you pick this place to look for them?'

'It's Marie Atkinson's cottage, isn't it?' I asked, and she nodded.

'Then that's the place I want. The diamonds are hidden round here somewhere.' My eyes narrowed suddenly. 'Have you seen Marie anywhere around?'

'I wouldn't know her if I had, but you're the first person I've seen since I left the village.'

'So she's not here now. Any signs that she's been around recently? Or that anyone's been in here?'

She shook her head.

I was starting to get worried. It looked as though Singer's bright idea could have been a dud after all, but I wasn't going to let it go as easily as that. There was nothing else I could follow up, no other lead that would take me anywhere near the diamonds, and staying here was better than wandering aimlessly around in that rain.

'Who told you about this place?' I asked. 'When you came to my flat you said that you'd never heard of Marie, yet now you're here at her cottage.'

'A friend of mine helped me.'

'Who?'

'You wouldn't know him.'

'Try me.'

'No. There's no point, and—'

I reached down and got hold of her shoulder. It was damp where the water had dripped off her face.

'Listen, Sandra,' I said savagely, 'there's you and me in here and all the row of that storm outside. Whatever I did to you wouldn't be heard beyond the garden wall, even if there was anyone around to hear it. You'd better make up your mind to talk as fast to me as you did to the cops when I wouldn't fall in with your blackmailing ideas.'

She didn't speak.

'Who sent you?' I demanded, letting her

drop at the same time.

She rubbed her shoulder.

'If you must know, his name's Rupert Singer.'

I felt like screaming. After a few seconds the impulse faded and I had an irresistible desire to laugh. She watched me and then said:

'What's funny?'

'Is that his real name, Rupert?'

She nodded.

'Is that why he's so interested in Rupert Bear?'

'Could be,' she said indifferently. 'What's that got to do with it?'

'Probably nothing. It's just interesting, that's all.'

I shivered with cold again and it struck me that it mightn't be a bad idea to do something about it. When I moved away from the girl she watched me but made no attempt to get up off the floor.

'Look,' I said, turning to face her, 'we're both here now and we're stuck until it stops raining. There's no point in arguing so much, is there?'

'That depends what you want.'

'I want the same as you,' I said roughly. 'The diamonds.'

'They aren't here!'

'Skip it for now,' I said impatiently. 'Is there any tea or coffee around?'

She nodded sullenly.

'I brought some with me in case there was nothing here that I could use.'

'Then make some. I want to try and get dry.'

She got up slowly, looking at me all the time as though she was waiting for the catch. She gave me the impression that she thought this was a trap and she was only waiting for me to hit her again. More water dripped from her, and she wiped it away with the back of her hand.

While she was making the tea I stood looking out into the night. It was pitch dark out there and I couldn't see a thing, but it helped me to get my thoughts into some form of order. Singer knew about her. I certainly hadn't told him, and if he'd only read the newspaper accounts all he should know about Sandra Howell was that she was the bird who'd been at Bannister's. He should have no reason to think that she might be up to anything on her own account, nor could I see why he should tell her that the diamonds were hidden here and then come down himself with me.

My unease deepened, and I was more than ever glad that I'd given him the slip and reached here alone. At least there was a possibility that I'd get something like a sensible story out of her before he arrived, and then I could deal with him in the light of what she told me.

A few minutes later we'd both had a turn of the towel that was in the primitive bathroom, there were steaming cups of tea and more in the big tea pot that she'd found, and things were something like civilized. It didn't seem to be raining quite so hard outside, and but for the fact that there was a fear of Singer turning up present at the back of my mind it might almost have been pleasant.

'Tell me about Singer,' I said, sipping the tea.

'What's it got to do with you?' she demanded. 'What do you know about him?'

'Never mind what I know,' I said. 'Just tell me what you know, and snap it up because he might be here at any time and I want to have the picture clear before he comes.'

'Rupert might come?' She sounded practically dull-witted, as if the mention of his name had frozen her mind.

'Call him Singer,' I said. 'It doesn't make me want to laugh as much. He gave me this address and said that I might find the diamonds here. He wanted to come down with me to look for them but I managed to give him the slip. That doesn't mean he won't turn up later, though, nor does it mean that the cops won't come after him.' I had a sneering look on my face. 'But that won't matter, will it? They're mates of yours, according to what I've seen in the papers.'

She flushed.

'Perhaps they wouldn't be quite so matey if they knew you were down here looking for the stolen diamonds,' I went on, 'but don't worry. Just tell me what you and Singer were up to.'

Unexpectedly, she giggled.

'I can't tell you all of that, and I don't suppose you'd be interested,' she said. 'He was my boyfriend. I didn't realize until after the robbery that the only reason he'd got friendly with me was so that he could pump me for information about Charles Bannister and the set-up in the house.'

'Just a minute,' I interrupted. 'If Singer was your boyfriend, what were you doing at Bannister's that night?'

She hesitated.

'I'd been working late and he let me stay the night.'

'It depends what you call work,' I said. 'What did you do when you realized what Singer was really after?'

'It was too late to do anything,' she said, 'and I don't think he knew that I'd guessed it, either.'

'Until you went to put the black on him,' I finished for her. 'You're a scheming little minx, aren't you?'

'I've got to get money somehow,' she said, as if that excused everything. 'What would you have done in my position? Bannister was dead, so I didn't have a job, and I wanted money.'

That situation was a little too near to home for me to be able to say anything.

'Let's not get onto that,' I told her. 'What did Singer do when you tried to blackmail him?'

'He played it better than you did. He gave me some money there and then, not as much as I'd asked for but enough to

keep me quiet, and then said that he'd
been double crossed out of his share of
the diamonds. He didn't know where they
were now, nor did he know much about
you, because his contact was a girl called
Marie Atkinson. His story was that he
didn't know how much you were involved
until he read it in the paper.'

'Go on,' I said impatiently when she
stopped speaking for a moment. 'Why did
he spin you that yarn? And did you fall
for it?'

'I fell for it,' she said bitterly. 'I started
to work with him when he said that it
would be too dangerous for him to start
asking questions about you in case you
had contacts in some gang or other. I said
that I'd find out who you were. I went to
Christie, like I told you.'

'Did you tell Singer you intended to
blackmail me?'

She nodded.

'I said that we could work together on
that. When I came to your flat and you

told me more or less the same story as Singer I didn't know what to believe. You could have been bluffing, Singer could have been lying, or you could have been working something between you, some plan to deal with me. Singer had said that either you or Marie must have the diamonds, and when I came to your flat again two days later and you'd gone I decided that you'd been bluffing to give yourself time to get away.' Her voice changed slightly. 'If I'd seen you then, I'd have killed you!'

'Get on with it now,' I suggested, jeering at her.

She didn't try.

'I was a bit afraid of going to see Singer again because I still wasn't sure whether or not you were working together, and I decided that the best thing was to tell the police everything, just as I'd threatened.'

'Not quite everything,' I said.

'What do you mean?'

'You didn't say you were doing it out of

spite because you couldn't blackmail me.'

'I'm not stupid. I didn't say anything about Singer, either, and a day or two later he rang me up. I don't know if you know how charming he can be when he wants—'

'I hadn't noticed it.'

'Well, he can. He convinced me that what he'd told me was right, and he just happened to mention that Marie owned a cottage in Cornwall. He arranged for us both to come down here and have a look.'

'When were you supposed to be coming?'

'Tomorrow,' she said, after biting her lip.

I laughed. She glared at me and I thought for a minute that she was going to throw her cup at my head.

'Singer played you for a real sucker, didn't he?' I said. 'He knew that if he fixed that up, and really convinced you that the diamonds were here, someone with your mentality wouldn't be able to resist getting here before him and trying to cheat him.'

'How did you get mixed up with him again?'

'Never mind that,' I said. 'All you need to know is that he also fixed up with me to come down and look for the stuff. If I hadn't got away from him we'd all have finished up here together.'

'But why?' she demanded.

'And where are Marie and the diamonds?' That was more important, to my way of thinking. 'You say that you haven't seen anyone else here?'

She shook her head.

'No signs that anyone's stayed here during the past week or so?'

'No.'

It didn't look too good. I finished the cup of tea, poured myself another and gulped that down. It was still scalding hot, and made me feel a lot better.

I said: 'What I think Singer wants is for us all to get together here and fight it out amongst ourselves for the diamonds. Afterwards he'll walk in and take the lot for himself.'

'You mean he wants to kill both of us?' she asked, her eyes wide.

'And Marie too, I should imagine. I guess I can read him better than you, Sandra, and that's the way I work it out. He won't share those stones with anyone, nor will he want anybody left around who'll talk to the cops.'

'But—'

'And he's on his way here now,' I said with a mirthless grin. 'When he gets here we're going to have to tell him that there are no diamonds and that they've never been here. There's about as much chance that he'll believe that as there is that Father Christmas will turn up instead of Singer.'

She bit her lip, but didn't say anything.

'He'll tear us apart if he thinks it'll help him to find out what we've done with them,' I went on. 'It's my guess that you're the one he'll work on. I bet he could hurt you a lot with those big hands of his.'

'And what'll you be doing,' she cried, her voice screaming and wailing in competition with the wind.

'Nothing,' I said flatly.

'You can't sit back and let him do things like that, can you?'

'I won't be doing anything because I'll be dead. There'll be you and Singer on your little ownsome, and Singer as mad as a coot because he thinks you're holding out on him. It'll be a swell party. A pity I won't be around to watch, because I'd like to see him giving it to you.'

'But I don't know where they are!'

'Tell that to Singer.'

'It's the truth!'

'You'll be screaming a lot louder than that before he's through,' I jeered, but personally I was starting to believe her.

I wasn't underestimating what Singer might do, but my real intention in building him up to look like a one-man inquisition had been to get her to tell me if she'd already found them. From the way she was behaving, though, it was fairly obvious that she'd no more idea where they were than I had, and that left us in something of an unenviable position.

'Look, Sandra,' I said, 'I know you're a creep and all that but I don't want to see you get hurt. Why don't we go out to my car? That way, at least we'll see him arrive, and when he does we won't be bottled up in here.'

She grimaced at me. The wind was howling, the rain was rattling against the windows and the waves were booming at the foot of the cliff. It didn't take too much imagination to work out what conditions were going to be like outside.

'Come on,' I said.

'But what are we going to do when he comes?' she asked, panic in her voice.

'We'll work that out when we see what happens.'

There was always the chance that he

hadn't managed to bluff those cops, of course, and they were still holding him; knowing Singer, though, I thought it more than likely he'd have got his story fixed up and we could expect him any time in the next hour.

When he arrived, the trouble would start.

'I'm frightened,' Sandra said, coming close to me.

'You can cut out that sort of act,' I said roughly. 'We're both in this against Singer but that doesn't mean we've got to like each other. Personally, I'd see you go over that cliff and not think twice about it.'

She stepped back as if I'd hit her. Her eyes were glittering, and her hair, still damp from the sponge, was slicked back to her head at the front.

'I'd rather take a chance with Rupert Singer than you, thank you!' she cried.

'Don't be so bloody stupid,' I told her wearily. 'If you stay here—'

I never finished that sentence. Clearly,

above the sound of the argument and the wind and rain and waves, came a shrill scream.

II

Sandra stared at me, her face white and her eyes burning out of it like coals.

'What was that?'

'Probably a gull fed up with the rain,' I said uneasily.

'Don't make me laugh. That was someone screaming, out there on the cliffs.'

'Then if you knew, why did you ask?' I snapped, feeling my skin start to crawl. The atmosphere of this place was bad enough without shrieks coming from the outside. I didn't feel like going to see what it was; there was too much chance of it being connected with Singer to make that prospect attractive.

Sandra crossed to the window, twitched back the curtain and peered into the night.

I joined her. The sky was getting faintly lighter, heralding the dawn, but apart from that we could see very little, and certainly nothing that would be likely to scream. After a moment she released the curtain and turned back to me.

'We'll have to have a look,' she said uncertainly.

'Yeah. Is there a phone in this place?'

'What do you think? You could be on a desert island for all the chance there is of getting in touch with anyone. If you want someone else here all you can do is go to the phone box in the village.'

I went to the front door and opened it. When I poked out my head I saw that it wasn't raining anywhere near as hard as it had been when I'd come in, although the wind was still gusting hard, driving the waves against the cliff. I went into the tiny garden, walked to the end of the path and looked over the gate. All I could see were the gaunt outlines of some scrubby trees, even the light of the ship at sea had gone.

Carefully, I opened the gate and stepped into the lane. There was no sound other than the faint grating of my footsteps. I shivered.

When I looked back to the cottage I saw that the door was still open, with Sandra standing there, outlined in the square of light. It would have been safer for her to either close the door or switch off the light, but that would have meant one of two things: either locking me out or prowling about in the dark. Neither of them appealed to me, so I didn't bother telling her she was a perfect target.

Just in front of me was the lane and at the end of that was the car I'd knocked off. If I chose, I could walk down to the car, get in and drive away. Apart from the immediate problems that wouldn't solve anything, and it would cost me the diamonds, but it was still attractive. If I hadn't started to think of them as my diamonds, something which belonged to me, and which it was right that I should have, and no one else, I might have done just that; as it was, I hesitated for only a second before turning the other way, towards that side of the cottage where I'd broken the window to get in.

Since that first scream there had been no other sound. I had nothing to help me in my search but the direction I'd thought that had come from, and in conditions like there were then it wasn't much.

The wind was blowing from the sea. That made it more likely that the person who'd screamed was over there, but while it was easy to think of prowling along the cliff edge, it wasn't so easy to forget that there must have been something to cause the scream.

The idea of meeting Rupert Singer on the crumbling edge of a storm-lashed cliff in the dark didn't appeal to me in the least.

Come to think of it, I wasn't keen on meeting him at all.

There was nothing round the side of the cottage as far as I could see, which wasn't far, I strained my eyes into the darkness then went over to the broken window. Through it I could see into the kitchen, through the open door and into the living room where we'd been talking, though Sandra was nowhere in sight.

I put my mouth as close to the jagged edges of the glass as I dared and shouted softly:

'Sandra!'

There was no answer.

'Sandra!' I cried, speaking more sharply but still keeping my voice down.

I saw her shadow fall across the doorway and then a scared white face appeared, looking towards me. Her lips tightened when she saw it was me but before she could speak I said:

'Is there a torch anywhere?'

'Frighten me to death next time,' she said bitterly. 'Don't think it worries me if—'

'The torch,' I said. 'And get a move on with it, it's wet out here.'

'There's one in my bag,' she said, and went back into the other room. Her bag was in the bedroom, which was where she'd got the tea and stuff from earlier, and it struck me now when I got back from poking around a good look at that bag wouldn't do any harm. It was too late to start now, of course, and I waited impatiently until she got back, expecting to see Singer at any moment.

The rain, a light drizzle, was worse than the pelting storm; it was so fine that it penetrated everywhere, soaking me before I realized it.

Near me, something moved.

Anyone whose nerves weren't pulled as tight as mine would have said it was the wind rustling something in the garden, but I knew better.

Someone was nearby.

I looked round cautiously, then I heard the sound of Sandra returning to the window. Whatever happened I didn't want the person who was in the garden to know that I'd heard him, so I merely grinned at Sandra when she gave me the torch.

'I don't know whether or not it'll be good enough for you,' she said.

'Never mind that, it's my worry,' I whispered. 'Stay in here and wait. I don't want you blundering around and confusing things.'

'Don't worry,' she told me with a shudder. 'You won't get me out there.'

As soon as she'd gone I whirled and flashed the torch. In spite of what she'd said about it, there was a good strong beam, but it didn't show me anything I didn't expect to see. Keeping it switched on I prowled slowly towards the garden gate.

No one moved. Apart from the low moaning of the wind, everything was quiet. There was a glow in the sky as the dawn crept nearer, making it lighter than ever, but it still wasn't easy to see things; once or twice I stopped abruptly, straining my ears, but I couldn't pick out that noise again. I had the impression that there was a darker patch of night over to my left, but when I looked more closely I saw that it was a bush, and snapped off the torch.

Angrily, I shook myself.

My nerves were too taut. If Singer had reared up at me from the ground right then I don't think I'd have been able to do anything but gape at him. Still heading into the wind, towards the sea, I moved off again; while I might not be able to find the joker who was moving about near me, I could probably discover who'd screamed as at least I knew which direction to go in. There was also the advantage that if the prowler thought Sandra was alone in the cottage it might tempt him to try his luck there; if he did get in, she'd scream fast enough and I could soon get back.

The disadvantage was that he might try to sneak up on me first, but that was something I put out of my mind.

I flashed the torch again.

Behind me, someone moved.

I whipped round but I was too late and there was only the empty path with the cottage at the end of it, the front door now closed. From here, too, I couldn't see any lights, and it looked as though the place was deserted. If Sandra had lied to me, and this was some plot to get me out of the cottage while she got away with the stones ...

But how could she have arranged the scream? She couldn't. She hadn't had any warning that I'd be coming; as there was no phone at the cottage not even Singer could have got a message to her, and he was the only one likely to know that I was on my way. Assuming that she'd had someone with her when she'd come down, why should they be prowling about on the cliff? It didn't make sense and it meant that there must be someone else here, someone who was a threat to both of us and would have to be sorted out before we could go any farther.

I was getting very near to the edge of

the cliff by this time, and I had to use the torch to make sure that I didn't slip over. The light made a perfect target, but by flashing it on and off and moving quickly in between the flashes I didn't do so badly.

In this way I found the steps. They weren't masterpieces of step construction, just roughly hewn things in the cliff. Curiously, I flashed the torch down them, trying to see where they led. The beam ended in a wall of darkness; if I wanted to find out anything more I'd have to go down them. I hesitated. The scream could as easily have come from here as anywhere else. After a quick look round to make sure that no one was sneaking up on me I started to climb down, moving very carefully on the wet rock.

The ground was very slippery, and crumbled a little under my feet. There was nothing between me and the sheer drop down the cliff face, either, so I pressed right against the rock, testing the surface before

I put my weight on it, kicking some loose stones out of the way at one stage, and shining the torch as far ahead as the beam would go. I reached the foot of the steps and began to go along what was nothing more than a ledge in the cliff, probably natural, with the steps cut some time in the past for ease of access.

Down below, the waves weren't breaking as savagely as they had been. The storm was over now, but that didn't mean it hadn't done any damage.

In front of me the ledge disappeared where the cliff loosened by the rain, had crashed into the sea. The ledge narrowed because of this; from being about four feet wide it dwindled to six inches or so, and even that didn't look safe.

There was no future in going on, so I turned back. All it wanted now was for me to find Singer behind me, but the steps were as empty as they'd been when I'd come down them. I reached the top, flashed the torch around, and still didn't see anyone, either prowler or screamer.

But for the scream and the fact that I was sure I'd heard someone moving I'd have called it a draw and gone back to the cottage. As it was, I couldn't leave it unsettled in case it affected what happened when Singer got here. It could have been Singer for all I knew, and brushing back my wet hair I stood undecided on the cliff top, the wind blowing off the sea and bringing the unmistakable salty smell to my nostrils.

To my left, something moved.

This time there was no doubt and I started after it. Now that there was something definite to work on all my nerves had vanished and the only thought in my mind was of catching the bloke I was chasing. He didn't look like Singer but I wasn't worried about that, either; once I had him in my hands he'd soon tell me who he was, and be glad to do it.

As I ran the wet, scrubby grass pulled

at my ankles, and once or twice I nearly fell; I saved myself, but the delay cost me a few seconds, and although I could still see a shadowy figure dodging from side to side he was getting further and further away.

To try and catch him I put on speed.

Then, I really did fall, sprawling headlong in the wet grass, the torch snapping off and flying out of my grasp. At the same time a sharp rock dug into me, but the thing that I'd fallen over appeared to be soft and solid at the same time, and the feel of it made my skin contract. I groped around for the torch. It didn't take long to find and the light came on as soon as I pressed the switch, showing me what it was that I'd been rolling on.

A body.

Marie ...

I leaned over her, trying to find out whether or not she really was dead, and then I knew that the man I'd been after had come up behind me.

'You won't find any diamonds on her, kid,' he said softly.

Turning, I saw Alf Christie.

Chapter Six

After that one sentence neither of us spoke for what seemed like a long time. Christie stared at me out of the darkness, his face apparently glowing in the light of the torch and giving the impression that there was just a head on its own, come to haunt me as a punishment for walking out on him that time. Gradually I realized that was why the person I'd been chasing had looked vaguely familiar; but for the darkness and the fact that I hadn't been expecting to see Christie down here I'd probably have recognized him earlier.

Had he made Marie scream?

Had he killed her?

Or was Singer also running around, confusing everyone and waiting his moment to strike at each one of us when we were least expecting it? My nerves prickled again, then Christie said:

'Aren't you going to make any comment, Wayne?'

'I've nothing to say to you,' I growled, pointing the torch down at Marie.

She was certainly dressed for the weather. Jeans, a longish raincoat and even one of those plastic rainhats, something which I'd never known her wear before. The bloodstain on the front of her coat looked almost black, but there was a subtle quality about the way it looked, which meant you couldn't mistake it for anything other than blood. She'd been stabbed, but there was no sign of the knife.

Christie was still smiling crookedly.

'Why did you kill her?' I asked, keeping my voice down for some reason.

'Not me, kid.'

'But—'

'Why should I want to do that?' he asked, interrupting me.

'How am I supposed to know that?

There's only the pair of us out here and I know I didn't do it. That only leaves you.'

'I don't know that you didn't kill her, do I?' he asked, raising his eyebrows. 'That makes us all square, doesn't it, kid?'

His white hair was plastered to his head. Rain was running over his red face, and he looked even more uncomfortable than I felt myself. Flashing the torch on and off and trying to see if Singer was anywhere around I peered into the darkness, but I could see nothing.

Christie's gun jabbed into me painfully.

I started round to face him, my breath hissing sharply.

'If I'd wanted to kill her,' he said softly, 'I'd have used this gun. Wouldn't I?'

'Not if you wanted to keep quiet,' I objected, my voice thick and hoarse, hardly able to form the words. 'That makes too much noise.'

Christie shrugged.

'Where's Rupert Singer?' he demanded.

233

'Somewhere the other side of Exeter, I hope. That's where I last saw him, talking to the cops.'

'The cops?' he asked, stiffening. 'What have they got to do with it?'

'There was an argument with them. I suppose Singer will manage to talk his way out of it.'

'Double-crossing him, eh?'

'Not as much as Marie double-crossed me,' I retorted. 'Where are my diamonds?'

'Your diamonds? Don't you mean Bannister's diamonds?'

'My diamonds,' I said savagely. 'I've done more than any of you to get those stones. I want them.' I started forward, but the gun jabbed again, bringing me up short. Angry though I was, you wouldn't get me arguing with a gun.

'Let's talk in the cottage,' Christie said. 'We'll be more comfortable there, even though it has stopped raining.'

We walked slowly over the springy grass, me holding the torch and Christie following, so that he could keep an eye on me and jab me with the gun whenever he thought I'd slowed up too much. From the frequency of the jabs I guessed that he was nervous, but I couldn't see any sure way of turning that to my own account, and besides, there were too many questions which I wanted answering before I started anything funny.

We reached the front of the cottage. Light flooded from it like a beacon, and when I stopped in front of the closed door Christie said:

'Got a key, kid? Marie had ours and I don't intend going back to look for it.'

'I got in through a window,' I told him truthfully. From the way he'd spoken I could tell that he didn't know about Sandra. That was probably something I could use if I could only see how, but before I had a chance to do anything there was a sound of movement from inside and then we heard Sandra's voice.

'Is that you, Wayne?'

'Who's that?' Christie hissed into my ear.

'A friend of mine.' I looked over my shoulder and grinned at him. He frowned.

'Get her to open the door,' he said. 'And if there's any attempt at a trick you're the one I'll shoot first, so you'd better be careful.'

'It's only me,' I shouted to Sandra. 'Open this door and let me in out of the rain.'

It opened slowly, as if she suspected a trick without even being told. When she saw me standing there she actually gasped with relief, pulling the door open wider. Suddenly her eyes looked over my shoulder and I could tell from the expression which came into them that she'd seen Christie. She moved back a pace and then looked stonily at me.

'What kind of trick's this?'

'No trick,' I said wearily. 'Watch him because he's got a gun.'

Christie clumped into the cottage after

me and back-heeled the door closed. It slammed loudly and Sandra jumped.

'Another of your girlfriends?' he sneered to me.

I frowned, then remembered that when she'd gone to his office to get my name and address she hadn't seen Christie himself but some young kid who was working there. Neither of them had seen each other before, though from the look on Christie's face he was slowly realizing who she must be.

'Is this the kid who gave all that stuff to the cops?' he asked.

'That's right,' I nodded. 'Her name's Sandra Howell. Sandra, this is someone you've heard a lot about, Alf Christie, my old boss.'

'Christie? Then where's—'

'Singer?' I shrugged. 'God knows.'

'He's here somewhere,' Christie said. 'He killed Marie.'

'Are you sure of that?'

'I guess so, because I don't think you'd

have the guts to do it, even after the way she's treated you.'

'Now look—'

'You're doing too much talking,' he said curtly. 'Sit down.'

He waved the gun towards one of the easy chairs. I sat in it and Sandra flopped into the other one. Christie stood near the fireplace, where he could keep an eye on both of us, and was so far away that trying to jump him and get the gun would be a suicide attempt. He grinned then, and smoothed his hair down some more, so that it looked as though someone had taken a nice, rosy apple and painted the top third of it white.

'How come you're here?' I demanded. 'Were you working with Marie all along?'

Christie nodded.

'We pulled so much wool over your eyes that it's a wonder you don't look like Father Christmas, isn't it?'

'Cut the funnies,' I said. 'If Singer turns up now you'll have your hands full dealing with the lot of us. Don't you think you've taken on too much?'

He nodded thoughtfully.

'It looks to me as though there's been some cross words between you two and Singer, but why are you working with Sandra? If she's the one who grassed to the cops about you I'd have thought she'd have been poison to you.'

'She is, but I've no choice. When I was working for you, did you deliberately try to put me off Marie?'

He nodded.

'We've been working together on jobs like that Bannister thing for a long time, and there've been some nice pickings. Marie's trouble was that she was scared of being caught, and I think that was why she was cooling off. I thought that if she started going around with you it might make more complications than I could handle, so I did my best to head you off.'

'Didn't manage very well, did you?'

'Maybe not. When you suggested pinching those diamonds Marie saw it as the way out of all our troubles. Singer had done work for us before and wouldn't make any difficulties about getting the information, you'd do the job and Marie and I would cut the pair of you out, split the proceeds and then retire. Neither you nor Singer would have had any come-back and even if you had it wouldn't have mattered because you wouldn't have been able to find us.'

His eyes went to Sandra who was watching him constantly, her gaze fixed on his face as if she thought they were the most marvellous features she'd ever seen. Though from the expression in her eyes she was actually thinking something quite different to that.

'I suppose I spoiled that plan when I killed Bannister?' I asked.

He flicked his eyes back to me.

'That's about it,' he agreed. 'We had the diamonds but things were different then, because there was a murder rap hung onto them and too many people who knew the truth were running around. The ideal would have been to knock you and Singer off, but we thought that would be too risky and all we could do was carry on more or less as normal until things quietened down and the cops stopped probing around.'

'And while you were doing that I suppose Marie hid at your flat?'

'She did in the end, but before that she came down here to get rid of the diamonds,' he said. 'Even if the cops had known that she was involved there was no way of proving it without finding those diamonds in a place where she could have hidden them. They wouldn't have found out anything about the cottage, and—'

'They could have done,' I said. 'Singer found out, and what he can do I'm sure the cops can, as well.'

'But they still wouldn't have the diamonds,' he said.

'Why? Where did she hide them?'

'We'll come to that later.' His eyes

glazed slightly and then returned to normal. 'When the days passed and nothing happened we reckoned we'd got away with it. Then when I came back from lunch that day the kid I'd got in your place mentioned that a bird had been in asking for your address. I knew that there must be some connection between that and the diamonds, of course, but there was nothing I could say to him, nothing I could do other than wait, because I didn't know who the girl was.'

'I'll bet you found that a hot time?' Sandra said.

'Not really. Even if they'd got Wayne and he'd named Marie they couldn't have done a thing because there wouldn't be any proof. What we'd have done would be to say that she used to be his girlfriend and he was merely throwing accusations around because he was jealous of the way she'd started going with me. Simple, isn't it?'

'You're a swine,' I said softly.

He shrugged.

'As you will, kid. This bird puzzled me for a while, but then I saw all that bull in the papers.' He grinned. 'If I turn you in now you're worth five thousand quid to me, and there isn't a thing you can do about it.'

The worst part of it was that he was right. If he handed me over to the cops now, I could tell them anything I liked about him, and even assuming they took me seriously enough to go into it there wouldn't be a shred of proof. More than likely they'd simply think that I was raving about him because he was the one who'd caught me, and it wouldn't get me anywhere. I moved slightly in my chair, and his finger tightened on the trigger.

I sank back.

The only good thing about it was that if he was going to do that he wouldn't shoot me.

His eyes were glazed again.

'But,' he said, 'the diamonds are worth thirty thousand quid. Why should I risk

243

what you might say to the cops about me for another paltry five thousand?'

I ran my tongue over my lips.

'I could kill the pair of you,' he said, 'and there wouldn't be anyone to talk then, would there?'

'Except Singer.'

'I can handle Singer.'

'Why did you come down here,' I asked, 'if Marie was hiding at your flat? Don't tell me you're psychic and you knew the diamonds were in danger?'

'It isn't as simple as that,' he said. 'Someone phoned up yesterday and said you'd discovered that Marie owned this place and guessed that the diamonds must be hidden down here. They said that you were already on your way. It could have been a hoax, I suppose, but if it was, then the caller knew a damned sight too much.'

'So you came to find out what was going on?'

'We guessed in the end that it must

have been Singer, though he disguised his voice well,' he agreed. 'If that was so, we couldn't afford to ignore it.'

'And didn't you suspect it might be a trap?'

'We did, but we still couldn't let it go. There was thirty thousand quid at stake.' He paused. 'How did you find out about this place?'

'Singer told me,' I said mildly. 'His game was to get the lot of us down here, let us fight it out and then walk in and take the pickings. If I hadn't fooled him he'd be here now, but as it is he's on his way. I think that he's finally got here, killed Marie, and he's only waiting for the chance to kill the rest of us.'

'I can handle him,' he repeated, though there wasn't as much confidence in his voice as there had been. 'He'll have to find out where the diamonds are before he kills me, otherwise they'll be lost for good.'

'Where are they?'

245

'You'll never know,' he declared. 'You'll be dead long before Singer gets to you.'

There was a slight noise outside. All our nerves were on edge and the effect was as if a stick of dynamite had exploded in the doorway. We all turned at once, then before I could take advantage of the situation Christie was staring back at me. He seemed to have forgotten about Sandra. She jumped up and hurled herself at him in the same movement.

He fell backwards under her weight. The gun went off. I'd been moving forward and the bullet skimmed me so closely that I felt its heat against my face. By the time I'd recovered from the shock they were writhing on the floor, with Sandra on top and seemingly winning.

'Bitch!' Christie screamed. 'You're after the diamonds, too!'

Sandra hit him again, then gouged her nails into his face so that he screamed.

'I'm going for the cops!' she shouted. 'You hear that! I'm sick of the lot of you and I'm getting out. I'll tell them that you brought me down here because you thought I knew too much about you.'

As she tore herself away from Christie I made an ineffectual lunge at her. The bullet shock must have affected my nerves slightly, because although I'd normally have caught her easily this time I was nowhere near fast enough. My fingertips grazed her, and then she had the door open.

'Sandra!' I yelled.

Her footsteps clattered down the path, towards the lane and the stolen car. I started after her, then paused. Even if I caught her, Christie would have had time to recover by then. By staying here and beating out of him where the stuff was hidden I could have it and be on my way long before any cops arrived. First of all Sandra would have to get to the village and find a phone, then there'd be the delay while the men actually made their way here. Unless the diamonds were hidden in some really bad spot that was almost impossible to reach there'd be all the time I needed.

I swung round.

Christie was reaching for the gun, which had rolled across the room; I stopped him by the simple method of standing on his hand, then grinned when he yelled out with pain.

'Different now, isn't it?' I said. 'Where are my diamonds hidden?'

'Your diamonds?' he jeered. 'You'll never get them, because—'

I pressed my weight onto his fingers again and his words choked off into a gasp. Casually, I leaned over and got the gun. After a quick glance to make sure that there were slugs in it I pressed it gently against the side of his head and told him not to move.

He lay absolutely still.

'Right,' I said. 'This is the position. Sandra's gone for the cops, and you know as well as I do that when she says that she means it. She threatened me with that when she was trying to blackmail me and everything you read in the papers arose because I thought she was joking. When she says she's going for the cops she means it, but they won't be here for about half an hour. I want to know where those stones are, and I want to know now.'

He grinned up at me. His mouth was the only part of him that moved.

'Even if I tell you, you won't believe me.'

'If you make it good enough I will,' I said. 'If you don't, then you're in for an uncomfortable half hour, and when I hear the cops arriving I'll shoot you. You won't die right away but they'll be too late to save you. Make up your mind, Christie.'

To emphasize my point I screwed the gun barrel into his ear, watching him suck in his cheeks as it bored into his head.

'I'll tell you!' he gasped painfully. 'You'll never get them but I'll tell you.'

'Well?'

'They're on the cliff path,' he said. 'If you find the steps and go down them and along the ledge for a couple of hundred yards there's a small cave. The stones are hidden behind a big rock at the back of the cave.' He grinned. 'See what I mean? Knowing that doesn't do you any good at all, does it?'

I didn't see in the slightest what he was getting at. I was about to give his ear another good poke with the gun when the meaning of what he'd said hit me.

The diamonds were at the end of that ledge. During the night the storm had washed away most of it and it was as he said. There was no way at all that I could get my diamonds back.

II

He laughed. The threat of the gun must have unhinged him a little, because the situation he was in and the expression on my face were certainly nothing to laugh at.

'There is no path now,' I rasped. 'No ledge and no path at all.'

'The rain washed it away,' he agreed. 'If it hadn't I'd have been away myself by now. You don't think I'd have been so stupid as to hang around if I'd been able to get the diamonds, do you?'

He wouldn't. I knew that, and it was what finally convinced me that they were really at the end of that path. I had to find some way of bridging that long gap which the storm had made, and I had to find it fast, before the cops could get here.

I was so busy worrying about that, and trying to work out a plan, that I forgot about Christie. Suddenly, he gave a violent heave, throwing me backwards. I saved myself by slapping the palm of my hand onto the floor, but by then it was too late and he was on me, his hands and fingers clawing at my eyes. I tried to fight him off but he had tremendous strength. I was on the floor, Christie was astride of me and the fingers were gouging into my throat.

I tried to say something about the cops, but the words came out in a strangled grunt that could have been anything. The pressure he was putting on increased relentlessly and I could feel something getting tauter and tauter in my throat; very soon it would crack, and that would be it.

My groping hand found the gun.

I shot him in the side of the head.

As he fell I caught him and lowered him gently to the ground. I don't know why I did that. Then I moved away from him, still holding the gun and taking care to avoid the spreading pool of blood on the floor.

The fact that he was dead meant nothing to me. If I hadn't shot him he would certainly have killed me, or handed me over to the cops and got his five thousand quid; he wouldn't do either of them now, and while I wasn't actually glad that he was dead, it didn't worry me.

All that worried me was the diamonds.

My diamonds, as I'd come to think of them after all I'd done to get them. If they were hidden at the far end of that ledge on the cliff I was going to get them, no matter how I crossed that gap. Right then I'd no idea what I was going to do, and before I made up my mind I wanted to have another look at the situation and see just how narrow it was where it had been washed down.

There was Singer to think about, too, but I pushed him out of my mind; with only about twenty minutes to go before the cops came there wasn't time to think about anything other than the diamonds.

I went outside. Because the light had been on in the cottage I hadn't noticed how rapidly the dawn had come up. The rain had stopped completely now, the clouds were clearing rapidly and the wind was dropping to a light breeze, making it a beautiful morning. Later, when all the clouds had dispersed and the sun was high in the sky, it would be baking hot.

Just the weather to enjoy having thirty thousand pounds worth of diamonds in your pocket.

There was no sign of Singer.

I hurried towards the cliff edge, retracing the way I'd come with Christie behind me. The grass was still beaten and flattened where we'd walked and when I passed Marie's body, halfway between the steps and the cottage I shuddered. All the feeling I'd had for her had long since gone, but that didn't mean I could enjoy the sight of her dead. Singer must have killed her, of course, but I couldn't see him, and I certainly wasn't going looking for him.

The only way down to the ledge was by the steps; there was no other way at all of reaching the far end, unless you counted things like winching a man down at the end of a rope from a helicopter. He wouldn't have had to worry about the path being washed away, but obviously that sort of thing was out as far as I was concerned.

Going down the steps, I walked as far as I could along the ledge.

In the dawn light I could see the waves, about a hundred feet below me, washing over the part of the cliff that had fallen into the sea. Half hidden by the water was a straggly bush; that must have gone down with the cliff and now its branches trailed limply and flopped about when the waves caught them.

The sea itself was a brilliant blue, and the contrast with what it had been like when I'd first arrived here couldn't have been more remarkable. The morning sun glinted off the white topped waves. The roaring and crashing had died down to a low murmuring. The sea breeze was gentle and refreshing, not a howling gale as it had been.

There was a gap of about fifteen feet in the ledge, and even for thirty thousand pounds worth of diamonds I wasn't prepared to risk jumping that. Frowning, I looked at it more closely and saw a very narrow ledge, about six inches wide, running right across the gap and looking about as safe to me as the lions' den must have done to Daniel. If I took it carefully I might be able to walk along it, but the slightest mis-step would send me plunging into the sea, even if the extra weight didn't bring the rest of the path down.

I tested it, very carefully.

Nothing happened.

Trying not to look down I turned my back on the sea and pressed myself against the damp rock, edging off the main path and onto the narrow strip, then moving step by step across the gap. It was worse than anything I'd ever done. Sweat began to pour off my face. A third of the way along there was a slight tremor of the rock and some pebbles and stones dropped into the sea. All my nerves cried out to me to hurry up and get this over with but I knew that if I did it would be the last thing I'd ever do, as apart from the fact that I'd be more likely to bring everything down that way, I'd be almost certain to slip before I was across.

More stones fell into the sea. Because of the noise of the waves I couldn't hear them hit the water, but I could feel them breaking away under my weight, and that was worse.

I reached the middle and paused. This was taking me a lot longer than I'd anticipated, and if I didn't hurry the cops might be here before I could get away; if I did hurry, I'd most likely kill myself. Depending on the size of this cave, there might be a chance of hiding in there without being found; after all, they didn't know about the cave because Sandra hadn't been there when it was mentioned, and one look at that gap would convince them that no one could cross it. I might get away with it, but I didn't really want to spend any more time than I had to fooling about on the cliff, and once they got here it might be hours before they left the area clear enough for it to be safe for me to come out again.

I began to cross the rest of the gap. Before I'd gone very far I knew that this end of the ledge was much more crumbly than the other part had been. Every step I took seemed to make it tremble and shake, and I finished up almost gliding across on my toes, hardly daring to lift my feet from the ground.

It didn't make much difference. I looked down. The sea appeared to be a long way off, and as the tide started to run out a narrow strip of sand was appearing at the base of the cliff. If I'd fallen into the full depth of water and not been hit by any of the rocks that I'd bring down with me and managed to avoid being buffeted against the cliff I might have survived; as it was, there wouldn't be much more than a foot or so of water by now, and I wouldn't have a chance.

The cliff trembled some more.

I began to take bigger strides. In spite

of myself I was hurrying, anxious only to leave this death trap before it gave way and took me with it, not really caring what happened when I got to the other side. The rock against which I was pressing myself was lumpy and cold. Every so often, a bigger lump of rock than usual meant that I had to lean backwards, over the sea, and that was worse than ever.

I made it at last.

As I stepped onto the full width of the path again I was surprised to find how much I was trembling. Wiping my forehead with my sleeve, I wondered if there was time to sit there for a few minutes, then decided that I didn't dare delay any longer. Only a few yards away I could see the dark opening of a cave in the rock but as I started to walk towards it I felt the now familiar tremors in the ground.

I stopped instantly.

There was a rending crack, followed by a crashing, roaring sound and clouds of dust.

I thought I was going with it, but as the rumbling echo died away I knew what had happened. The narrow ledge that I'd just used must have given way under the strain, and I was trapped, with no way back.

Slowly, I turned round, hardly able to bring myself to look and confirm my guess.

Singer was standing at the other side of the gap, a look of terror on his face and a gun in his hand.

III

I stepped back, pressing myself against the rock face just like I had when I'd been coming across the narrow gap. The part of the path that I was on curved round slightly here, and I knew that he couldn't reach me with a bullet from where he was standing. The path must have broken away when he tried to follow me across, and in one way that was good; if he hadn't tried it, it would have collapsed when I'd attempted to get back.

I had Christie's gun in my pocket, but there was no point in using it yet.

Singer still looked terrified.

'Hard luck, Mr Singer,' I shouted.

I saw his lips tighten. He raised the gun, but all I did was laugh.

'Unless you can shoot round corners you won't get me here,' I jeered. 'I wouldn't waste bullets.'

'Where are those diamonds, Edwards?' he yelled. 'I suppose you thought you were smart at that cafe?'

'I take advantage of things, that's all.'

'I convinced them you'd picked me up on the road,' he said. 'I thought I wasn't going to manage it at first because that counter hand said he thought we were too friendly for that, but they had to believe me in the end because there was no proof.'

I was getting Christie's gun out of my pocket.

'Held me up for a long time after,' he

went on. 'Giving a statement, trying to remember for them if you'd said where you were going. I even had to make up a description of the gear I said you'd stolen off me when you'd driven off with it still in the car. As soon as I could I pinched another one and got after you.'

'A pity,' I told him. 'What are you going to do now?'

'Wait here for you,' he said. 'You'll have to cross back to here sometime.'

That shows you how stupid he was. The path had fallen away completely for six or seven feet, it was impossible to jump across safely, and any attempt would bring more rock down. In spite of that, he was going to wait there until I came back.

'How do you expect me to get back?' I demanded.

'You'll find a way,' he said casually.

'Sandra's gone for the cops,' I said. 'They'll be here in a few minutes.'

'She won't go anywhere near a cop.'

'She's done it before,' I reminded him,

'and I'd be willing to take a chance that she'll do it again. Don't forget that if she spins them a yarn that satisfies them she'll get five thousand quid from Charmwear.'

In my heart I knew that she'd do it, too; even without past experience to go on the sound of her shrieking voice when she'd said it would have told me that. I wasn't going to waste time trying to convince Singer. Whatever I said, he wouldn't believe me, and anyway he'd find out soon enough without me having to do a thing.

'Why did you get us all to the cottage?' I asked. The gun was right out of my pocket now, and I was holding it out of sight.

'I want those diamonds,' he said. 'I knew they'd be here somewhere but I could have spent weeks looking for them and not found them in the end. Even if I had, there's still have been too many people wandering around who knew all about me. I guessed that if I could get you all here together you'd argue amongst yourselves and save me a job.'

He hadn't been far out, either. Apart from Sandra there was only me and him left, and we knew where the diamonds were.

'I listened outside the cottage,' he went on, 'and heard you talking to Christie. After you'd killed him I followed you to here, but as soon as I tested that ledge with my foot it crumbled away to nothing.'

'Not such a smart punk as you thought, are you?' I said, stepping right out into the open and raising the gun.

I squeezed the trigger.

It had jammed.

Before I had time to do anything a slug whipped over my head and smacked into the cliff. I tried to fire again but it was jammed solid and there was nothing I could do. Tossing it into the water I turned and walked away.

The cave was smaller than I'd expected from Christie's description, just an over-grown rabbit hole about four feet across. I peered into it, wishing that I'd thought to bring the torch with me, then shrugged. I'd nothing to lose, and I didn't think Christie had been making it up.

It was a tight squeeze, but once I was inside the walls opened out quite a lot, smooth looking, almost as if they'd been part of some ancient tin mine, in use when mining techniques were still being invented. I stayed with my hand on the rim of the opening while I peered into the dank gloom, which smelled of salt and seaweed. At the back was the big rock which Christie had mentioned, but when I went over to it and leaned on it there was nothing more certain than that it hadn't been moved this side of the Dark Ages.

Crouching, I felt around it. There didn't seem to be anything hidden here at all, and I was starting to think that Christie had played a last joke which was grimmer than he'd realized when I saw the edge of something white, tucked between the rock and the back of the cave.

Trembling again, I took it out.

It was a box, wrapped in a piece of white cloth which turned out to be that torn shirt I'd worn on the night of the killing. I opened the box and saw the washleather bag inside, full of diamonds which glittered slightly even in the blackness of the cave.

They reminded me of a lot of things. The time I'd first seen them glittering in Bannister's place when I'd barged in past Sandra Howell. The way the first safe had been empty when I'd unlocked it, and then how I'd found them upstairs. They'd glittered again, then, the moment before I'd heard Bannister sneaking along the passage.

All this had come from that ...

If I'd been a few minutes earlier or later at Bannister's on that first day, none of this might have happened. That was a comforting thought because it made me out a victim of circumstances, but I knew that it wasn't true. I'd wanted money, and if I hadn't got it from these diamonds I'd have got it some other way, probably with much the same result in the end.

Leaving the box and the torn shirt on the floor of the cave I squeezed out into the early morning sunlight again, swinging the washleather bag from my hand.

It was full of diamonds. My diamonds. Even Bannister hadn't done as much as I had to earn them.

Singer was where I'd left him, standing there, glaring towards the cave. When he saw me he lifted the gun, but from where he was there was no way in which a bullet could hit me, and I wasn't bothered.

'I've got them,' I said. 'My diamonds.'

He stiffened, and I held up the bag so that he could see it.

'All I've got to do now is get back to safety,' I went on. 'As far as I can see, there's no way of doing it.'

'You'll find a way.' His voice was harsh. 'We'll split them. Equal shares.'

I laughed.

'Even if I could get back I wouldn't split

them with you,' I said. 'They're my stones, Rupert. Mine.'

I sat down on the ledge, leaning back against the cliff. The sun was fairly high now and I poured the diamonds out onto the rock, poking them with my finger so that they glittered and twinkled.

'You have three quarters of the money,' Singer yelled. He was glancing back over his shoulder now, and I knew that he shared my belief that Sandra had meant it when she had said she'd go for the cops.

'No,' I told him. 'If I can't have them nobody will. Not even the cops when they get here.'

He stared at me, a puzzled expression on his face showing that he didn't know what was in my mind, and adding to the enjoyment I was getting from playing with him.

'Did you stab Marie?' I asked him.

'She got in the way. I'd have shot her but it would have made too much noise. That was the only slip up I made, because I'd have rather one of you had killed her.'

'Too bad. You should have let me know and I'd have seen what I could do.'

I prodded the diamonds again, letting them roll around, shining and twinkling like silver plated beetles.

'Listen—' Singer began.

I interrupted him.

'When the cops come they'll be able to get you for killing her, won't they?'

I lifted one of the diamonds, pinching it between my finger and thumb and letting the sunlight reflect off it. As I moved it about, Singer's eyes followed it, like a cat with a ball of string.

I smiled at him.

'If I can't have them nobody will,' I repeated, and tossed it lightly over the edge of the cliff.

He yelled something but I didn't hear the words. I simply sat on the edge of the path pitching diamonds out to sea one by one. When I was three quarters of the way through the heap Singer shouted:

'They're coming, Edwards. I can hear the siren.'

He turned and began to run as swiftly as he could, back towards the steps. I watched him, then picked up the remaining diamonds and tossed them all out to sea. As they fell they made a final sunburst of glittering lights, a dozen shooting stars falling from the sky, a dozen hopes vanishing into the water for ever.

'It won't be long now!' I yelled after him, and settled back to wait.

This Large Print Book for the Partially sighted, who cannot read normal print, is published under the auspices of

THE ULVERSCROFT FOUNDATION

THE ULVERSCROFT FOUNDATION

. . . we hope that you have enjoyed this Large Print Book. Please think for a moment about those people who have worse eyesight problems than you . . . and are unable to even read or enjoy Large Print, without great difficulty.

You can help them by sending a donation, large or small to:

**The Ulverscroft Foundation,
1, The Green, Bradgate Road,
Anstey, Leicestershire, LE7 7FU,
England.**

or request a copy of our brochure for more details.

The Foundation will use all your help to assist those people who are handicapped by various sight problems and need special attention.

Thank you very much for your help.